RESISTANT

RESISTANT

A Novel

RACHAEL SPARKS

Published by SparkPress, a BookSparks imprint,
A division of SparkPoint Studio, LLC
Tempe, Arizona, USA, 85281
www.gosparkpress.com

Published 2018
Printed in the United States of America
ISBN: 978-1-943006-73-1 (pbk)
ISBN: 978-1-943006-74-8 (e-bk)

Library of Congress Control Number: 2018942982

"When It Don't Come Easy"
Lyrics and Music by Patricia Griffin
Copyright © 2004, Almo Music Corp. on behalf of itself and One Big Love Music
Used by Permission. All Rights Reserved.

Book design by Stacey Aaronson

For M, R, and W, who always believe in me,
and Rube, for telling me I was capable of more.

A mighty creature is the germ,
Though smaller than the pachyderm.
His customary dwelling place
Is deep within the human race.
His childish pride he often pleases
By giving people strange diseases.
Do you, my poppet, feel infirm?
You probably contain a germ.

—Ogden Nash

TABLE OF CONTENTS

 PART ONE

 PART TWO

PART THREE

 PART FOUR

PART ONE

No Medicines Left

CHAPTER 1

Stevigson Farm, Woods Hole, Massachusetts,
November 2041

The thermometer on the window read ninety degrees Fahrenheit, enough for Rory to suspect that the typical afternoon power outage would arrive soon. Outside, the leaves on the trees were barely turning yellow at the edges, hinting at the start of a fall that wouldn't get crisp for weeks yet. At this temperature, her research thesis would have to take an extended hiatus. Their solar panels were broken, and rolling brownouts were a common occurrence. She wanted a break anyway. Evenings felt cooler if you hadn't been inside all day.

She saved her work with a quick tap on the hologram screen and then tapped it again to close. The projected screen and keyboard disappeared, leaving only its small flat bar. It was an outdated holo-laptop, but it worked well after she had traded computer repairs for a bushel of potatoes with a traveling electrical engineer who was passing through Woods Hole.

Yanking on boots, she headed downstairs to the back porch and out toward the orchard. Its apple trees, fruit weighting the limbs and near harvest, filled almost an acre of their farm and were a good source of income. But the apples were also a great deal of work to haul in, and that was before the labor required to make chips, jam, and cider to sell locally. Rory had always found their spindly, droopy branches rather creepy, but she admired their durability in the face of several shockingly hot winters and a few freak blizzards.

She found her father past the orchard in the back acre, where rows of wheat were also days from being ready to harvest. The crop would yield just enough for a few bags of flour. It was getting so expensive to buy now that the Midwest had reverted to dust-bowl status. He was proud of this first year's crop, but she wasn't keen on learning how the thresher worked.

"Aurora Rosalind. Goddess of the dawn and the harvest!" her father shouted in a mock blueblood Boston accent.

"Lord Byron, fair rogue," she called back with a deep, mocking bow. "I thought I'd check on you before I go check the crab traps." She reached him where he was pulling weeds from the row edges.

Her father was a tall, lanky man with a crop of sandy blond hair growing coarse with age. Dressed in his standard hat, overalls, boots, and T-shirt, he looked far more like a farmer than a doctor of science in climatology and the author of two published books. Three more books still languished on the holo-laptop for the time when the world cared again about reversing climate change. *Too late to reverse*, he liked to say. *The earth already reversed on us. We just need to stay ahead of its inhabitants now.* Of course, after the die-off, all her father really meant was the microscopic inhabitants. Even one of their own tiny family had fallen victim to bacterial resistance to medicines. Rory's mother was three years gone, but the pain still woke her with nightmares.

"Crab for supper again? Catch me a lobster for once, will you?"

"Get your boat working again, and I will," she retorted.

"I'm a meteorologist with a pitchfork. You're the smart one."

"I'm a microbiology student with a crab trap." She squinted at him, but secretly she loved these games. Since they'd lost her mother, these teasing moments revived her in their memories.

"You're a doctoral candidate with a master's in bioengineering and a minor in biochemistry. Make it run on potato peels," he said. She was already heading away toward the docks.

"I'll get a real doctorate just about the year that a seventies-era marine engine can be converted to biofuel."

"Got your knife and Mace?" he called after her with a father's worry. Rory waved a hand up that gripped her knife without turning around, and then she hooked it onto the back of her belt.

Byron watched his daughter walk away, now at twenty-three as tall as her mother and just as lean as he. Her hair was darker, wavy, its length bouncing against her back as she walked. He could still see the toddler version of her, walking hand in hand with her mother, always curious, forever trying to pocket or eat whatever she found. She still had the curiosity, the resilience she'd shown then, traits her mother, Persephone, had passed on to her. More than she realized.

The die-off had left them with little more than their wits and the land they owned, but Byron knew how valuable their wits really were. With the population cut by almost 15 percent by the time Rory was seven, and no antibiotics developed yet to combat the resistance of every common bacterial enemy of humans to the antibiotic medicines available, survival skills seemed as valuable as job skills. They still had minimal infrastructure—even electricity and internet most days—but nobody needed a climatologist to tell them that Woods Hole, Massachusetts, was exhibiting the weather he had grown up around in his Raleigh, North Carolina, childhood. They had made a decision, as a family, to turn this family vacation spot into a real farm. It had felt less like a sacrifice than a strategy. Then Persephone had left them, a victim of the very bacteria she had long struggled to develop medicines against. Right now, he couldn't tell if they were winning. But he suspected that the long game rarely felt that way.

CHAPTER 2

US Army Task Force for Epidemiology and
Antimicrobial Research (TEAR) Laboratory,
Bethesda, Maryland

The team of eight researchers around the massive conference table worked on their laptops in impatience, reviewing their presentation. Their coffee was ice-cold by the time their audience of three finally arrived. Everyone was on their feet, as if they'd instantly been drafted and suddenly knew how to salute.

"General Kessler," the lead scientist greeted the tall, barrel-chested general with black eyes and a close crop of pepper hair.

"Dr. Rajni," he said with a brief handshake and a glance over the other seven scientists. General Bill Kessler didn't like doctors. He needed them, but he didn't trust or like them.

Rajni couldn't remember the other men in uniform but nodded respectfully and said, "Officers, please sit."

"Yes. Let's make this efficient. Tell me when we'll have anti-body stock."

Silence filled the room like smoke, and Rajni glanced back at his team to encourage them to begin the presentation. From the center of the round table, the holo-projector sent a column of soft light up through the center of the room, and an image of a 3-D, multiheaded, multicolored blob appeared to float in the center. It stuttered, disappearing for a few moments while the scientists frantically tried to restore it.

"I miss the days of projectors and flat screens," Kessler sighed. "Hologram laptops, hologram projectors—why can't we just fucking project onto a wall or use a damned screen instead of dust mites?"

The holograms suddenly reappeared, now sharp and visible as their light sources illuminated particles in the air and earned an unimpressed huff from Kessler.

Clearing his throat, Rajni—looking a decade older than his forty-five years—pointed to the blob as it began to animate, moving in space toward an oblong, elliptical body that appeared in the animation. He pointed to the elliptical shape.

"That is a bacterium with the pan-resistant antibiotic resistance genes, able to resist all our existing antibiotics. This, to the side, is an antibody from within a healthy, immune-competent individual who was able to survive infection by a pan-resistant bacteria." As he further narrated, the antibody latched onto the bacterium, and another larger cell body soon appeared, matching up to exposed sites on the antibody, then quickly engulfing the whole combination. "In a normal, healthy person with the ability to survive—"

"Dr. Ranji, we've seen this all before," interrupted Kessler. "We know how survivors' immune systems work, how the mac . . . macrama . . ." He waved a meaty hand.

"Macrophages?" the doctor supplied.

"Yes. Macrophage immune cells from our bodies eat the bacteria after the antibodies latch on. I need to know what you've engineered for the rest of us who are lucky to have survived this long without being exposed. What's next." It was an order, not a question.

Ranji looked over at his team and nodded, and they nodded back. Now the animation showed a differently colored antibody attaching to the bacteria. Nothing more happened.

"Despite numerous promising approaches, the antibodies either directly from donors or from mouse and synthetic models were successful at receptor binding sites either in vitro or in vivo, but phagocytic cell response is lacking or insufficient to reduce the burden of pan-resistant- gene-positive cells enough to allow survival. The donor models seem to be the only models where receptor binding is successful in triggering the full immune cascade that will allow for defeat of a pan-resistant bacterial infection."

"You mean . . . it doesn't work?" Kessler squinted angrily.

Rajni nodded. "I mean that the antibody latches on, but the macrophages don't finish the kill. Put simply, for whatever reason, the bacteria infecting the victim do not die. Instead, the victim dies. Dr. Simon can provide more detail on the reasons we suspect for failure."

A young black woman stood up and wrung her hands as she spoke. "We've examined the receptor binding in the donor survivor blood and haven't yet been able to identify the unique parameters that create a positive-binding and subsequent immune cascade environment. It's not simply the antibody alone. Some other unknown factor seems to be at play."

"Maybe the antibodies are not binding fully?" suggested one of the officers, who had a bachelor's degree in biology.

"We've ruled that out as a possibility. Binding is successful and abundant."

"Are they on some sort of . . . I don't know, special diet? Vitamins?" Kessler barked.

Dr. Simon shook her head. "We've controlled for such factors. There are no special reasons that we can identify why the donors work and the others don't."

Kessler practically growled in frustration before a fist came smashing down on the table. "There are hardly any donors left! It's been almost four years and seventy million dollars—you've probably bled them dry already! How in the holy fuck have you all screwed this up so badly?" He surged to his feet. "You're supposed to be the best goddamned researchers in the world!"

Dr. Simon visibly trembled, but Rajni was cool and composed.

"The best goddamned researchers in the world," he said, his mild Pakistani accent the only thing to betray his discomfort, "are mostly dead. We're what you have left, and we are just as upset at our lack of progress."

"Well, who the fuck is going to figure this out? The world is waiting to attack us, and we've got half the military defenses we had fifteen years ago. Who do I need to hire?" Kessler bellowed.

Rajni shrugged. "There is no one. I think only my mentor could have solved this."

"Who? Where is he?"

"She. Dr. Persephone Tyler-Stevigson. She's dead. She died over two years ago when we were beginning to make progress." He looked down, overcome for a moment with regret as he recalled their last words.

"She's dead." Kessler visibly regained control over his temper, glancing at his officers. "That's terrible. I'm sorry. Did she die here?"

Rajni was silent.

Dr. Simon spoke up. "No. She had decided to go back to her family farm and take care of her husband and daughter." She paled when Rajni sent her a quelling glare.

"Ah. One of those survivalist types," Kessler replied smugly. "Not in the Midwest, I hope."

"She was from Woods Hole, Massachusetts," Rajni said quietly. "She cannot help us now. We must keep working and hopefully try to discover more donors who haven't self-reported their infection survival."

One of the officers leaned across the table. "We've given you every donor we have. We've scoured the nation. Do you think they're in hiding or otherwise avoiding detection?"

A young doctor from the group cleared his throat, and the officer's instant glare in his direction caused a nervous pause before he explained, "Probably, though not intentionally. Our data are just too fractured with lack of complete reporting. So many hospitals and medical examiners have closed, and their mortality data weren't reported to the CDC. We lack a nationalized database of survivors—that is, survivors who actually contracted a resistant infection and managed to recover. If such a database existed, well . . ."

Dr. Rajni completed his thought. "We wouldn't be needing to meet."

"Explain."

"General Kessler, we've discussed this before. We really lack the epidemiological data to reveal the most vulnerable populations.

It seemed intuitive when the elderly were the most commonly infected, but then the bacteria transferred the antibiotic resistance so successfully across species that there was no most-likely-to-be-infected type of patient; everyone seemed equally at risk. We need to know what is in common amongst survivors, and our current pool of donors is not revealing any clues. We can't take the handle off the pump."

"What?" Kessler snarled again. "What pump?"

Rajni shook his head sadly. "Sorry. It's an old epidemiology term. Dr. John Snow, the father of epidemiology, famously ended a cholera outbreak in London by removing the handle from the water pump that he suspected was the source of the outbreak. It ended the cholera epidemic." He sighed. "But we have no such easy answer."

A silent miasma of tension, sadness, and frustration filled the room. Kessler nodded with finality: the meeting was ended.

"Keep working. We'll find more donors."

All the scientists glanced at each other uncertainly, not understanding that they were dismissed. Rajni gave them a toss of his head toward the door and they all filed out, Rajni closing the door behind him. The bacteria animation hung frozen in air over the center of the table before the military men.

Kessler took a deep breath. "I want eyes on the farm of that dead doctor—Staig-whatever?"

"Persephone Tyler-Stevigson," his officer read from notes on the table.

"Right. Eyes on the farm immediately. Maybe the family knows something. Maybe she kept working."

"Eyes on the farm. Yes, sir."

Hibernia Wind and Energy Farm

In the control room, a young man with a patchy beard sat before a computer and pointed to the screen.

"So the database she's been working on, for her thesis. It's really surging. This idea of hers for a crowdsourced reporting portal, it was nothing short of brilliant. From what I can tell, even kids are getting involved as, like, miniature science projects. Within a couple months, maybe less at this pace . . . it could yield some interesting insights."

His small audience of one woman and two men nodded in agreement but didn't comment.

"How much attention is it getting otherwise?" one asked.

He looked to the woman who posed the question and tried to read her flat, controlled expression.

"Well . . . I only monitor traffic, not IP sources. I could run a—"

One of the men interrupted him. "Run it. Cross-check against all concerned parties. Tighten surveillance. And get eyes on the ground in Woods Hole. Now."

CHAPTER 3

Stevigson Farm, Woods Hole, Massachusetts

A massacre of crabs, potatoes, and corn lay out across the porch table, a few shrimp shells in the mix, between Rory and Byron. Byron had opened beers for them—another handy skill he'd taught himself upon arrival at the farm—while they watched the sunset over the wheat fields.

"Did I tell you that new registrants at the database jumped fifty percent last month?"

Byron looked over in shock. "Really? From all over or just one pocket?"

"All over," Rory nodded. "I'm up to twenty-seven hundred nationwide. I might be able to report something preliminary soon for the thesis."

"Wow. That's worthy of a cheers!" he grinned, clinking his bottle to hers. "Oh, I almost forgot something special I got you. I traded with Kathleen Stewart, who dropped by while you were out getting the crabs." Leaning back to the satchel he carried on the farm, he produced two bright orange, kidney-shaped items not much bigger than crab apples.

"Mangoes?" Rory breathed out disbelievingly. "Dad, that's amazing. I miss mangoes so much."

"Well, save the seeds. We'll put them in some compost and start a grove. Who knows—they're probably in the right climate now!" he chuckled.

She kissed his cheek and sat back to admire the fruit as if it were a gold-and-diamond necklace. "Some people have a hard time keeping such a positive outlook, you know. On my site, in the forums, I had to add an FAQ about why we don't count loss due to suicide."

Byron sent her a sidelong glance but let her finish without clarifying.

She continued, "Too many kids out there have parents that gave up, without even being infected. They lost so many of their own, or maybe they needed insurance money. It's amazing you're able to stay so positive."

Byron took a long breath in, then out. "When your mom and I were kids—before we even met—we knew it was coming."

Rory's head whipped around. "How?"

"John Donne once wrote, 'There is no health; physicians say that we at best enjoy but a neutrality,'" Byron recalled, and Rory glared at him for a more serious answer. "We were smart. Like you. We read. We paid attention. History warned of it, current bacterial evolution was a huge red flag. I think that a lot of people knew. They just didn't want to believe it would be so bad. But when it began . . . Persy and I admitted to each other that it was no real surprise. The only surprise was that it wasn't us. Some people turn to religion in hard times, and we, well . . . we turned to each other. And science. It helped us cope. Helped us prepare and survive." *And helped us prepare you.*

Byron took a long sip of beer. Fireflies began to flicker in the early dusk, flirting with each other among the plants. "I've never liked the idea of suicide. But then, I've never been in as terrible a spot as people who consider it. It's probably as much a genetic risk as a social one."

"You mean the propensity toward it just . . . isn't in some people's makeup?"

He shrugged. "It's hard to prove or disprove a negative, but yes, that's my suspicion. So when I say this, I say it with a disclaimer of my own ignorance: at this point, no matter how bad things are, there may be more opportunity than there ever was before. More opportunity to survive, to flourish, to do better than our forefathers. That's how I want you to approach life." He took another swig before rummaging in his pocket and producing a harmonica.

"Dad. Really?" she sighed.

"Practice makes perfect."

"You're perfectly awful."

"Get your fiddle."

"I think we scare the chickens."

"No, they like to hum along."

She gave a dramatic sigh and went inside, returning with her violin. Perching on the porch table, she ran the bow across the strings, wincing at the first couple notes before she felt the training kick in and the notes fall into her mind, aligning with the whine of her father's harmonica. At the height of their song, a howl picked up in the woods not far away, nearer to the marshes. They both paused, turning to smile at each other.

"He's back," Rory whispered.

"See, we have one fan."

Rory woke before sunrise the following morning to a clear, almost cool morning. As she gathered eggs from their few hens, she felt oddly anxious, as if she'd forgotten an important event or appointment for the day. It wasn't anyone's birthday that she knew, and the calendars didn't reveal any special events for the farm, but the nagging tension in her neck wouldn't ease, so she decided exercise was the best approach. Leaving a note for her father, she slung her backpack, loaded with water, a meal, and tools, over her shoulders, and then she headed for the eastern shore. A three-mile hike would be a good morning start.

About a mile into the hike, she began to wonder if the anxiety was intuition. She felt . . . watched. Stopping, she used the excuse of sipping some water to scan the tree line. Rory found her shadow lurking among small bushes, lying low, so she pretended not to see him and resumed her hike. Tracking him in her peripheral vision was difficult but possible, and he followed for another mile. At this point, it only seemed fair to give him a chance—he hadn't attacked yet, so perhaps he was friendly.

So she stopped, nearer to the trees, and sat on a rock. He watched, no longer bothering to hide. Rory pitched him a piece of her breakfast bread.

"I see you," she called, and the wolf stared back stoically. He kept his distance, but when the bread was thrown closer to him, he nosed forward and took a bite. She managed to tease him to getting about twenty feet from her, but then he suddenly caught wind of something, perked his ears south, and disappeared. "Next time I'll bring the fiddle," she chuckled as she resumed her hike.

By the time she reached the eastern docks, the sun was high enough to be blinding off the water, and the day was already warm. Her father's small skiff, proud but useless, still floated true at the small marina. *At least she's dry.* Turning potato peels into biofuel was unlikely, but she'd been reading up on small motors and had thought of a few repairs that might help it run again. Giving him back that small pleasure would be a worthwhile effort, and she cracked open the motor hatch and laid out her tools and notes like a lab technician setting up a new experiment.

An hour later, she had run through every creative curse she knew, motor grease was streaked to her elbows, and Rory was resolved to give up. Maybe she could trade some eggs with Jake Andersson— he always seemed handy with engines. Her neck prickled as it had all morning at the thought of him . . . he had such a creepy habit of staring.

If she could just get this gasket replaced, it might tell her the downstream issue in the motor, but reaching it required an extra elbow joint. Already she was sprawled awkwardly on her side, trying to find the leverage to loosen the gasket cover. It was too far for even her long arm. She pulled her knees up and tried to put her weight into it. With her left hand, she gave the stuck gasket cover one more attempt at loosening. Greasy fingers slipped, and her knuckles slammed into the engine block.

"Motherfucker!" she squeaked out through clenched teeth. Head down, pulling her arm back out, she lifted her eyes on another curse. A face across the bars of the stern from her—dark, male, and disfigured—had her jumping back in terror so abruptly that she knocked her head into the doorway to the hatch, and stars filled her eyes. "Oh, oww . . ." Rory moaned, holding her head and trying not to fall down the stairs.

"Are you all right? I'm sorry—I didn't mean to scare you." The man was suddenly aboard the boat, and though she tried to open her eyes, the pain was briefly so intense that she decided to just breathe carefully and calmly while she fumbled for her knife on the deck. A warm hand covered hers, placed the knife in her right hand, and folded her fingers around it. "It's okay, I'm not going to hurt you," he said simply, and she thought briefly that his voice felt like a tiger under a blanket.

She opened her eyes to see him crouched close, watching her with concern. Her vision was still a little blurry. She saw his eyes first, dark amber and watching her with an intensity that unnerved her. He looked only thirty years old, but strangely marked as if someone had tattooed or painted his face with indigo ink, once around his square right jawline and down his neck, and then again from his forehead down across and under his left eye to widen and wrap under his left ear. He wasn't disfigured, but he wasn't meant for magazine covers. His hair was short, almost military in its severity. His eyes looked genuinely concerned.

"Are you okay? I'm sorry I startled you. I was just going to offer to help."

She gripped the knife but nodded.

Rory sat back on her rear, her knees ahead of her and her knife across them. "Who are you?" she whispered.

"Navy." He offered a slight smile, and she got the impression he was out of practice at it. "You?"

"Rory." Taking a long, deep breath, she lifted her left hand and frowned at its odd shape. Two fingers lodged in an unnatural angle.

"That looks painful." Navy could see the skinned knuckles were only a minor injury; it was the two jammed fingers that would really hurt. "How do you do with pain?"

"I'm pretty tolerant. What are you going to—oh, my God! Oh,

fuck, *oww!*" Rory shrieked as he jerked her fingers back into alignment, and then she sucked in a violent breath between clenched teeth as the sharp stinging pain subsided into a dull throbbing ache. She exhaled slowly and focused on his again as he wrapped a bandana around her battered knuckles and tied it carefully. His eyes, amber brown and tinged with green, seemed to have a gleam of admiration. "It's really unwise to do that to a woman holding a knife in her other hand."

Navy nodded. "Fair point. But if you don't unjam them right away, the swelling makes it too painful later."

After another few deep breaths, Rory felt in control again, and her vision was clear. He couldn't help but respect her for managing her own pain that well, but he was still a little concerned that she'd given herself a mild concussion.

"All right, Navy. I guess you're just passing through?" She nodded to his large pack on the dock.

He sat back from her and pushed to his feet. He was tall, as tall as her father, and considerably stronger looking.

"Probably. Unless you're willing to pay for boat repairs."

She raised a dark blonde brow over blue-green eyes. "Where are you from?"

"I was in the military. Now I'm not."

Rory waited a beat, then stood. "I can't pay money, just food. I can't even promise you'll have a job, but we could use an extra hand at our farm for the harvest month. My father will need to agree."

Navy nodded at her understandingly. "I'd appreciate it."

Byron saw his daughter's arrival from a bird's-eye view of the farm. Repairing solar panels on the roof of their farmhouse gave him the altitude to view over the orchards and wheat fields to the pair approaching from the eastern shore. Using the folding binoculars he always kept handy, he examined their visitor closely.

Rory had always been a bit of a savior of injured birds. Thankfully she had no real idea of how helpful she could be to them, so he was able to limit her engagement with sick neighbors, ill or injured wanderers that floated up from time to time. If she had truly understood, he suspected her choice of doctorate would have been in direct patient care. Ignorance was more than bliss these days. It was protection.

Which was why the more-than-healthy-looking stranger striding alongside her was already causing the hairs to prick on Byron's neck. Aside from his bizarre choice in tattoos, he was tidy enough to seem like a salesman and carried himself with almost military bearing. No other visible tattoos revealed a loyalty or side interest, and his pack was as nondescript as his pants and shirt.

With a sigh, Byron soldered the last loose wire and headed down his ladder to meet them near the front poor.

"Dad, this is—" Rory began, but Navy cut her off.

"Afternoon, sir. I'm passing through and met your daughter by chance at the boat docks. My name is Navy."

Byron cocked an eyebrow at the name. "How eponymous."

Navy didn't acknowledge that with a reply, but blinked as if to say the joke hadn't gone over his head.

"Byron Stevigson." Byron let the quiet slowly expand in the warm air.

"Dad, Navy gave me a little help on the boat. He's willing to do more repairs, for room and board. I thought we might use an extra pair of arms with the apple harvest, maybe the wheat also."

Byron and Navy eyed each other. "Where are you from?"

"Maine. Among other places. I'm, um . . . retired military." Navy's voice dropped a register, but Rory couldn't read into his tone at all. She watched curiously as he and her father eyed one another as if they both were tailors sizing the other for suits. Rory had known her father too long to be intimidated by him, but she knew when he was applying those techniques to others. Navy, meanwhile, she found mildly intimidating just standing next to her. His size, his piercing gaze, and the dark markings across his visage were disarming.

"Rather young for retirement."

Navy nodded but didn't comment. "I'm happy to stop traveling a while and help, or to move on if you prefer."

Byron extended a hand, and Navy shook it firmly. Turning over the younger man's hand, he chuckled to himself and offered a smile. "You've got the hands of a lobsterman's son. They can leave a mean mark, can't they?"

Now Navy looked surprised, and a reluctant smile warmed his face. "Hurts like hell when they do." Watching him get caught by the surprise of his own grin, Rory felt a weird jump in her chest. He'd hardly said ten words on the walk back from the boat.

"Got a few of those scars myself. You can stay and help, in exchange for repairing the boat and helping around here. If I decide you're not helping, you leave when I say, and the rules are . . . whatever the hell I say when I decide to say it. Fair?" Even Rory was impressed with that policy speech.

"HUA," Navy said like a salute, abruptly respectful again. *Heard. Understood. Acknowledged.* "Where can I start?"

Byron's gaze switched to Rory. "Start by telling me why your hand is broken."

The first week with Navy helping was a pleasant shock for Byron and Rory both. While only asked to help with a few specific tasks, by his third morning with them, he was up before them both to take on chores they'd never asked him to do. Rory found him chatting with the chickens before sunup.

Coffee in hand, just out of his sight, she watched him examining the hens in their nests. His broad shoulders seemed tense as he crossed his arms and studied them. After a few moments of consideration, he cleared his throat and spoke, softening his deep voice a little.

"It's probably impolite of me to do this, so I'll just apologize in advance. I don't usually go prying into people's homes like this. But I'm pretty sure you don't have any need for these."

"You know, you don't have to sweet-talk them out of the eggs, right? They just plop out." Rory sipped her coffee as she watched him slip a hand under a hen's nether regions and smoothly turn up a bright gray egg. Considering the hand, she was frankly impressed the hen didn't seem to notice.

"Plop out. Technical jargon?" Navy guessed. "I was mostly just hoping to avoid being bitten."

"Pecked. The meanest ones lay the best eggs."

"How do you avoid drug-resistant salmonella? I thought I'd read that's a big problem."

Rory nodded. "It's more likely among large farms. We vaccinate, though."

He cocked his head without looking at her. "There's a vaccine for salmonella that works?"

She straightened abruptly, her coffee sloshing over the edge. "No. But I . . . I guess we've been lucky." In a smooth change of subject, she added, "The neighbors have, too, with our chicks. I should up the price." When he turned to watch her expression, she was gone.

He left to work on the boat after breakfast and didn't return until lunch. Rory was working the garden when he surprised her by kneeling down and starting to pull weeds. She had to admit, she wasn't sure if she'd expected him back, but he had left his pack inside the room they had given him.

"Oh. Hello."

"Hello."

"How are . . . things?" she chuckled when he didn't say anything to her.

"Fine."

"Navy, really," Rory laughed. "I've had barn cats more chatty than you."

He met her teasing smile with a flat expression. "You didn't hire me to chat." Rory was taken aback, but she couldn't quite look away from his eyes, that squarely locked jaw. The cruelty of the remark stung, and with her limited chances at social interaction, it hurt more deeply than she expected. She suddenly realized that she might be a terribly unappealing person to speak with. Who would have warned her?

"I . . . I'm sorry," she finally decided to say. *He was honest, why can't I be?* Rory thought. "You deserve to be paid better if I expect friendship."

His eyes never left her face, and the pain in her features and voice felt almost palpable to him. God, he was out of practice. It was so unusual to have someone react to him, to his face, without disgust. She resumed steadily pulling weeds, eyes down, radiating humility. Not judging him, despite how his words had hurt her. He didn't know for a moment if he'd ever seen a more beautiful woman in his life. Against all training, he reached out and covered her hand in his. Rory's blue-green eyes lifted. Unadorned. Unassuming.

"I'm sorry," he said, halting. "I just hurt you. I'm not accustomed to anyone being comfortable around me. Friendship with you isn't . . . It isn't a chore."

Rory could read more in his eyes, but she wasn't sure it needed to be spoken aloud. She smiled softly, looking back down to their gardening.

"Good. Because I'll warn you, kale is a chore to eat. You may wish you'd eaten the weeds later."

His laugh, barely louder than a deep breath that vibrated the air around him, sent a warmth down her spine.

That afternoon Navy found more wiring errors in the solar panels, based on a hunch that they were underproducing in wattage. He helped cook dinner that night and earned a beer for a thanks. Byron pulled out his harmonica, Rory reluctantly revealed her violin, and they played "Long Hot Summer Days." To Rory's surprise, Navy recognized the ancient lyrics and hummed along. The wolf in the forest howled along behind him.

"What was that?" Navy asked quietly.

"Our strong fan base," Byron deadpanned. "He's a red wolf. A little displaced, it seems, but he's been around for months."

Navy looked to Byron. "A wolf? Is that typical in this area?"

Byron shook his head and stretched his feet out to the porch railing. "So many animals are having to adapt to the climate changes, and it's far more difficult for them. We've evolved a whole level of technology to help us cope. They have nothing but their wits and muscles. Someday, many years from now, we might know how many extinctions were caused. It's probably thousands of species wiped out."

"Millions," Rory echoed quietly. When Navy sent her an incredulous look, she shrugged. "We used to be part of a network that helped track ocean life changes—whale migrations, shark sightings, tracking tags, fish catch, even plankton. The data hinted at a devastating impact."

Byron sighed and added, "Unfortunately, the gentleman who had organized the tracking network went dark about two years ago. We assume he was infected."

Navy cleared his throat, sipped his beer, and stared quietly toward the wolf's howl. They seemed knowledgeable about the predator, but he had learned only to trust upon close inspection. Drones no longer looked like his father's old model planes.

The week became a slow shock for Navy, too. It had been a long time since he'd had the satisfaction of doing a hard day's work for work's sake. Something about harvesting a turnip you ate that night or nibbling on an apple fresh from the tree imparted a sense of place that he only vaguely recalled from his childhood in Maine. Rory and Byron were a strange pair, but their unnerving brilliance was balanced with a humility and generosity that he'd never encountered before. Not many people accepted the appearance of his discolored face without some distaste, or questions, or natural human revulsion. They never showed any. He could tell they were curious, but they never asked. He learned that they traded frequently with neighbors, keeping their friends close by an economy of kindness and community. Rarely, they bought goods from stores, but seemed to avoid it and the legitimate currency it devoured. Their evening chats were often devoted to theorizing inventions that would solve problems of sustainability or reduce waste, but always keeping in mind how they could then be built and shared freely with others. Money or patents never entered the discussion.

Whatever his orders, getting to know them only reinforced Navy's suspicion that they were innocent in all this, and ultimately victims. It was hard to think of them in any other light.

CHAPTER 4

By Thursday evening, after working on it for the afternoon, he announced that he'd found the boat motor's issue.

"Really? That quickly?" Byron exclaimed.

"I think the leaky gasket caused a bit of corrosion down the line. I found some unused parts in storage at the marina, and by tomorrow I should be able to see if that fixes it."

"Now see, Rory. That's how you fix a motor. You could learn something."

Rory flashed a wry smile at her dad. "I'll stick to my own talents, but thanks. But maybe you can give me the abridged version of the repair tomorrow. We'll go put out a lobster trap," she said to Navy. He met her gaze briefly, his green-brown eyes seeming to hold a glint of hope and excitement that was out of character for him, but then he quickly found a piece of food on his plate that needed a glare. Rory didn't know what came over her, but she reached out and nudged his hard shoulder playfully. "I saw that, Navy."

One eyebrow, slashed by the dark blue pigment across his face, rose sardonically and dropped just as quickly.

"Saw what?" he replied without inflection.

"I saw that boyish thrill cross your face. You're so excited to throw out a lobster trap that you might go fix the boat tonight."

Byron watched the interplay with curiosity. He might not like it, but he had to reluctantly admire his daughter's skill at flirting. Her mother had been a killer at it, but she'd been able to go to college, to practice. Rory was an amateur, and Navy was already losing.

Navy sighed and leaned back in his chair. "I think you saw alarm." He waited a tense beat, frowning at her. "I've seen you on a boat, Rory. I'm not sure I have the first-aid skills to help you survive lobstering."

Byron let out a roar of laughter that was soon answered by a howl not far outside the house.

Navy helped Byron wash the dishes that night while Rory devoted time to her thesis, and he used her absence to probe into their past.

"When did she die?"

"We lost Persephone a few years ago," Byron explained. "We don't like to talk about it much."

"I'm sorry." Navy took a different tack. "Has Rory ever had an infection?"

"Nope. Very lucky there." Byron looked to Navy. "Your family?"

"My father died of an infection. My mother is still living. I don't see her much, but she seems safe every time we talk. My sister and her family live with her, in Maine. So . . . do you think living this kind of lifestyle, out in the country, is the key? Or do you guys have a secret sauce?"

"Secret sauce?" Byron laughed.

"Yeah, I mean . . . you're all three so brilliant. I would wonder if it's all luck."

Byron was quiet. "All three?"

Navy didn't miss a beat. "Rory told me your wife was an amazing doctor. A lead researcher. I didn't mean to upset you, sir."

"No problem, son," Byron sighed. "As much as I wish I could find a secret sauce, and as much as Persy tried, I don't have that answer tucked in a syringe somewhere. And if I did, I'd share it."

Navy let the quiet sit between them for a while. He believed Byron, for what it mattered to anyone. And Persy's work obviously lived on with them. But they weren't ready for what was coming. "Sir . . . about the wolf. I think it needs to be killed."

Byron stopped and studied Navy, who was steadily scrubbing an impossibly blackened pan. "Are you worried for Rory?"

"Yes. It could be hungry, dangerous. Desperate."

"Or hungry, lonely. Needy."

"It doesn't belong here. You can't predict its behavior."

"Sometimes I take a chance on those types of animals."

Byron woke late that night reaching for Persy. As usual, the point when his subconscious crossed the boundary into reality left him almost doubled over in regret and pain. God, he missed her. Sometimes visiting her headstone in the back of the property made him feel better, or perhaps it was just the walk. Either way, lying in bed miserable wouldn't fix him. He chucked on jeans, boots, and a shirt and headed out with a small flashlight.

The moon was almost full and lit the farm with that silver-blue that almost made it feel cool out. He was only fifty yards from the house when he saw the wolf, watching and tracking him from the far tree line. In the color-drained world, it appeared mottled gray, but its eyes picked up the light of the moon. It tracked him for a while and then dashed off suddenly into the trees. The dash gave him a surprise, made him pause. He stood still, the breeze carrying voices to him. He thought he heard Navy's voice, but he didn't recognize the second voice. *Is it Rory? Is this a tryst? God, being a father sucks sometimes.*

But it was a male voice. Instinct, for protection of their home and of Rory, had him sprinting toward the voices in the apple orchards. Navy sighted him when he was a dozen yards away, and Byron saw the dark-skinned, taller man standing across from Navy, but neither moved.

"Who the hell is this, Navy?" he demanded as he approached. Neither needed a flashlight to see the other.

"Mr. Stevigson, I—"

"I never authorized you to invite guests," he warned angrily.

"Yes, sir, and I'm sorry. This is my friend; he's also traveling by foot. He was a few days behind me and caught up."

Byron waited a beat. "Bullshit. He's been here the whole time."

Navy took a breath, squaring his shoulders, but gave a curt, honest nod. "You're right. I let him sleep on the boat. Neither of us is dangerous, I promise. This is Army." He gestured to the newcomer, a strong, tall young black man with a shaved head. When he smiled, his teeth practically glowed in the moonlight.

"Bullshit again. I want your real names."

"Unfortunately," the man answered with a slight accent, holding out his hand, "I don't know any other name. The Marines gave me that when they took me in as a boy from Trinidad. I don't recall what I was called before that."

Navy could tell Byron was too angry and uncertain to know what to ask next, and he jumped into the divide. "Byron, we're both just military grunts that got out after the government burned us. You can see my scars in the daylight. Army got his scars from the same people, they're just more subtle."

Army tipped his head to the flashlight clenched in Byron's hand. "You can see it, if your torch has a black light." Byron looked down at the small device, turned it on, and pressed the toggle button until a violet-toned UV light shone, making his white shirt glow in the darkness. He lifted it to the black man's face and nearly jumped as small, bright green stripes appeared on every bit of exposed flesh. It was as if his skin were lit from beneath. "I'm just glad they didn't call me Frog," he joked. His manner was friendly, more naturally extroverted than Navy.

Byron looked to Navy, who nodded with understanding.

"I realize I should have been more honest with you. Everyone who meets me is typically so repulsed that they never trust us at all. You and Rory, you surprised me. I didn't expect you to be so . . . different. Army is actually who fixed the boat."

Army laughed and punched Navy's shoulder with a force only a brother would permit. "Ah, you tried to pretend you know how to fix a motor? Now that's lying with flair!"

To Navy's surprise, Byron let out a reluctant chuckle, disarmed by his friend's natural warmth.

"Okay. I'm going to believe you. What caused this skin condition you both have?"

Navy glanced at Army and then met Byron's eyes. "We're not sure. We were told it was an experiment to create immunity—an ability to survive the bacteria. It failed, and the rest of the men in our unit died."

"We barely survived," Army added. "Don't know how."

Byron sighed and looked up at the moon, then down the rows of the apple orchard.

"All right. This discussion is by no means over, but I'm not in the mood for an all-nighter when we need to start harvesting apples tomorrow. You can stay, Army. But you'll work your ass off."

"Yes, sir," he said with a respectful salute. "And thank you sincerely, sir."

"Let's go."

They fell in line beside Byron and headed toward the house. Navy's eyes scanned the tree lines for the wolf. For any wolf.

"Maybe you can fix that broken Jeep for me, too," Byron suggested. When there was no answer, he glanced past Navy to their new guest. Navy cleared his throat.

"I already did," Army admitted.

As they neared the house, Rory rushed barefoot onto the porch with a flashlight, wearing only an oversized shirt. When she turned the light on and pointed it toward them, Navy realized the beam was trembling. He broke into a sprint to the house, taking the four porch steps in one bound.

"Are you okay?" he asked, grabbing her arms and running his hands down them to check for harm. "Was it the wolf?"

"What? No. Where were you? I woke up and everyone was . . . gone." Rory realized her voice was shaking and reined it in on the last word, trying to make it sound like a scold instead of a scare. She rubbed her arms where his hands had painted a trail of warmth.

He let out a breath he didn't realize he'd been holding. "We're fine. We . . . Your father and I took a walk. I'm sorry we scared you." Touching her felt so good, so reassuring, he had to clench his hands not to do it again.

"You didn't," she lied. "I was just surprised." She'd woken from a nightmare of being left alone on the farm, her father, the animals, and everyone else dead. *And you dead*, she thought. She didn't realize the tear tracks were still on her face until he ran his thumb over her cheek.

"You're crying."

"No, I'm not." She slapped the back of her hand across her cheek, squared her shoulders, and hugged herself to keep from hugging him. He was close enough that she could feel his warmth. "The doors were open, everyone was gone. I was just surprised." Her tone was meant to be light, flippant. It almost worked.

"You said that." He took her hand and rubbed his thumb over it. She looked up into his eyes again and desperately wished her father wasn't walking up behind him . . . with someone else?

"What the hell . . . ?"

Navy turned, releasing her hand reluctantly. "This is my friend, Army. We were in the same regiment. He's passing through, too. I just wasn't sure if you had space for us both. Byron says you do."

"If I work my ass off," Army quipped, then added with an outstretched hand to Rory, "Excuse my cursing, ma'am. It's late, but I should mind my manners."

She shook his hand hesitantly, still a little off-center after the fright. *After Navy's touch*, she thought. "Hi, um . . . Army?" It occurred to her that she was barely dressed.

"Check this out, Rory," her father said cheerily, then looked to Army. Game, Army grinned and nodded consent, and Byron flipped the black light back on to shine it at Army. As his face lit up, she tilted her head in sheer, curious amazement. Byron chirped, "It's some sort of mesodermal bioluminescence!"

Rory took in a slow breath, and Navy was the only one to notice it shook a little as she released it. "Army, welcome. I . . . We . . . um . . ." She struggled to find a proper welcome. "Oh, fuck it. I'm going to bed. I'll be polite in the morning." Turning on her heel, she disappeared up the stairs.

Byron watched in quiet amusement as Navy's eyes followed Rory every step until she was out of view.

"She's just like her mother. She'll make you coffee and break-fast in the morning, but *late* is not her finest hour. C'mon, gentle-men. We have a full day tomorrow."

CHAPTER 5

The day did start early with a pleasant breakfast, but Rory had little time to learn more about Navy and his friend's shared past before they were sketching out the plan for the apple harvest. Ripe apples and the storms Byron predicted would mean a great deal of lost fruit and income unless they were largely done with the thirty-odd trees by evening. If it was a lightning storm—more deadly since the climate had warmed—their window would be shorter. After explaining and demonstrating how their system worked, now much faster with a functional Jeep, Byron assigned Rory and Army to work the Jeep while he and Navy suspended the nets from the next trees.

It was simple physics: hang a circumference net from the widest limbs, shake each major limb to drop the ripest apples, and then pick the rest by hand. Ladders helped, but their trees were young and most fruit was within reach. And once Army got the hang of it, he was already thinking up new ways to move quicker. By noon, the limbs of over twenty trees floated a couple feet higher than before, relieved of their tart burdens. After a quick lunch, they dove back in as a breeze kicked up from the eastern shore, but by three in the afternoon a driving rain had begun.

With only three trees remaining, Rory wanted to slog through, but Byron shouted a different order.

"We still need to get everything into the barn and start sorting. Those will have to wait," he said, raising his voice to conquer the wind and clutching his hat to his head.

Rain was beginning to plaster her hair to her face, but Rory blinked it away and shook her head. "I'll finish, you guys go sort!"

Byron knew his daughter. "Fine. But don't blame me when

you're cold and wet and the water heater doesn't work tonight." She smiled and kissed his cheek, then jogged back to her trees. Navy, shaking his head at Byron's indulgence, gave Army a nod to the barn and followed Rory to help.

"You're stubborn as hell, you know that?" he shouted at her over the wind.

She shrugged and kept picking and throwing apples into the net. "It's important. This is our biggest income." Rain blinded her as she looked at the higher branches, then over to the Jeep pulling into their barn. *It won't get done by just looking at it,* she thought, and started to pull off her boots and socks.

Navy hadn't noticed until she was five branches high, plucking apples and throwing them like a spider monkey.

"Are you crazy? Get down, Rory!"

"In a minute!"

Lightning, unseen but heard, snapped a mile or less away, sending a shiver of warning up Navy's spine. "Get down now," he told her again. Lightning began to crisscross the horizon like a quilt of electricity.

"I'm almost done." When she glanced below, he was halfway up the tree to her.

"Rory, get the fuck down right now!" he roared, and her eyes widened. At that moment a blinding bolt of light struck the barn's lightning rod, and she let out an involuntary squeak. Shaking, she headed down the branches, and another splinter of light went into the forest to the west, just as close.

"Let go!"

Rory looked down at him, standing on the ground just beneath her and between two limbs she needed to reach to jump to the ground.

"Trust me and let go, Rory!" Navy begged.

Rory looked at the tree trunk, thought of what dying from lightning must feel like, then clenched her eyes and pushed away. Wind rushed past her ears for a couple seconds before she landed in his arms and opened her eyes.

"Well done," she smiled, but he wasn't amused. He set her down, and they crouched low and close to each other. About fifty yards of open field lay between them and the nearest structure, a storage shed tall and wide enough to park two cars under. Both sides had sliding doors.

"Is that place grounded?"

"All the buildings are." She could just see her father watching from the barn through the sheets of rain.

"We're going to run, but you need to stay beneath me. Ready?" She looked at him and when he met her eyes, it occurred to her that Navy was very nearly fearless. She nodded. Wrapping an arm and most of his body around her, he pulled her into a run in a bent position. A protective position. At the second they reached the shed doorway, one bolt of lightning shot down, forking right near the tree they had left as if to say, *I told you so.* Rory stumbled to her knees. She could feel the charge in the air raise the hairs on her arm.

"Let's shut the door," she said urgently.

"Don't touch them!" he thundered at her. Until then she hadn't seen how furious he was. "They have metal rails and handles." He glanced around, then grabbed a nylon rope from the wall, looped it through the door handle, and slid the barn door closed on their side, then went to the opposite. He could see Army and Byron watching anxiously from the main barn, so he sent Army a few hand signals. *Team okay. Hold for weather to wrap before moving.*

Army communicated back that he'd understood.

Rory sat on a bench to catch her breath and pushed her wet hair from her face. Navy paced back into the center of the building, lit only by an LED bulb above him.

She raised her face to look at him as she squeezed a stream of water from her ponytail. "Well, that was fun."

His eyes seemed to blaze. "Fun?" he repeated chillingly. "You could have died out there. What were you thinking?"

She shot to her feet, cheeks burning. "I told you: I was thinking about our income." To Rory, his anger seemed out of proportion to her crimes. He was practically vibrating.

"So you climb a tree in an electrical storm. Listen to yourself!" He grabbed her shoulders and gave her a slight shake. "How am I supposed to protect you when you act like that?"

"When did you become my protector? I've hardly known you a week."

In an instant he regained his control, released her, and stepped back. Rory's eyes narrowed. She stepped into the gap. "You're just passing through. You could be gone tomorrow." *And it would hurt like hell, and I would forever wonder why.*

"That was a stupid, stupid move out there."

"You're right." Rory tipped her head curiously. "And you saved my life. Why did you do that?"

"Anyone would."

"Doubtful. You told me to trust you and fall." She paused, stepping a little closer to him. She had to tip her head back to hold his eyes. "I trusted you, Navy. Why don't you trust me?"

Navy's hands felt on fire to touch her, to grab her, to absorb her into himself. She just stood there, ocean eyes full of complete, open, dangerous trust, her skin still glistening with rain. He couldn't control his reactions to her.

He gave in and wrapped his hands around her jawline. "This isn't about goddamned trust. I just don't want you dead." He kissed her, hard, almost punishingly pressing his lips to hers, but then her arms snaked around his shoulders and she pressed closer, opening her mouth under his. Some wall inside him crumbled. He gentled, wrapping his arms around her back and waist, gathering her as close as he could, and the slight whimper of pleasure that shivered through her practically snapped his last bit of control. He had to stop. End the kiss. This couldn't go further. He pulled back, but both of them were at a loss for breath, both shaken. Navy found that his self-control did not extend to releasing her from his arms, so he leaned his forehead against hers.

How do you undo me like this? he thought. His insides felt twisted up, and yet he'd never felt this good before in his life.

"Why did you trust me?" he had to ask.

She gave a little sigh and smiled. "Any man who talks to chickens before taking their eggs is a good man." Rory dealt in honesty, so she admitted the truth. "And because you climbed the tree to get me."

He chuckled, perhaps the first grin she'd ever seen from him. "I did. That was harder than it looked."

"It's easier barefoot." He leaned back to look down and saw her toes wiggle at him from the ground, eliciting another laugh. "You should do that more. Laugh. It looks good on you." She lifted a hand to touch his cheek, but he was suddenly kneeling down.

"Rory, you're bleeding." Her shin was badly scraped, enough to tear her pants, and blood had seeped through the ragged material. "Jesus. Is there a first aid kit here? You could get infected. We need to put some alcohol on this."

"It's okay." Dropping to sit, she let him roll up her pants leg and they inspected it. "It's okay. I heal quickly."

In a post-antibiotic era, where a mere ear infection could spell imminent death, her reaction was more than odd. She could see the questions in his eyes.

"First, leaving your body's own microflora on the skin helps signal to your cells not to overreact or get too inflamed. There's a complex interplay between the microbiome and our own cells."

"This is what your doctorate is about? The microbiome?" Reluctantly, he sat back, but he kept a knee bent beside hers.

She shook her head. "My master's degree and bachelor's. I didn't have the benefit of a big lab to study in, so the degrees are a little nominal." She brushed the dirtiest spot of her shin clean as she explained more. "But I suspect the bacteria we're all trying to survive . . . when we get a foothold in the battle, it will be because we came to understand a new definition of being human." His eyes held hers as he shook his head slightly in confusion. She smiled warmly, drinking in the details of his face close to hers. "Our bodies contain more bacterial cells than human cells. To say nothing of the billions of varieties of viruses floating everywhere. And perhaps some other categories in between that we just haven't discovered yet. We're not separate from our environment; we just evolved bigger. The line between human and bacterial is far more gray than some people are comfortable understanding."

The storm hadn't let up yet, and for a moment a clap of thunder shook the whole building. Navy eyed the rafters, trying to gauge the building's age and stability.

"Did you go to college before you joined the military?"

"I was studying to be an engineer in the military. I wanted to be a mechanical engineer." He was still staring up at the rafters, and she reached out and touched his cheek, her fingers tracing over the dark-blue-and-tan color of his skin.

"Why didn't you?"

"After the experiments, after Army and I escaped, it was more important to lie low. Registering at a college, trying to secure a job . . . they would have found us."

A deafening roll of thunder cracked, and they both flinched a little. Looking back to Navy, Rory shook her head.

"I don't understand. They want you back?"

He covered her hand with his on the hay-strewn ground between them and debated whether total honesty would harm or hurt her now. He decided to float the line.

"I'm not entirely sure. But we believe that if we were found and brought back in, we would be . . . lab rats. Whatever changed our skin may have also helped us survive the infections. But if it did, it was no miracle drug. We both barely recovered."

She seemed lost in thought for a second, as if solving a problem in her mind. A tiny wrinkle furrowed her brow, and her eyes seemed to glaze.

"Where did you go?" he asked, and she focused on him with eyes that made his palms itch to drag her to him again.

She didn't answer but shook her head. "You seem hale and healthy now."

"Notwithstanding your efforts at electrocution."

"Your chances at being struck were still at, like, one in a hundred."

He laughed, then asked, "How are you so fearless about that, but waking up alone made you cry?"

She glanced down and bit her lower lip for a second. "I'd had a nightmare. That I was alone on the farm, and everyone was dead." Rory met his eyes again. "That you were dead. I went to get a glass of water, and it was like I hadn't woken from the nightmare."

The laughter had left his eyes, replaced with a dark intensity.

"I won't let that happen." His hand cupped her jaw and he brought his lips to hers, this time with tenderness, kissing her gently and slowly.

Rory's mind was spinning when he pulled back and looked up toward the roof.

"Storm's passed." He looked back down at her and then tugged them both to their feet. Holding her hand, he sighed. "Listen, for Byron's sake—"

"Let's spare my father the reality of my adulthood?" she laughingly completed his thought.

Navy was chuckling. "Yes," he said in answer to Rory as he pulled open the barn doors and let the rain-cooled air sweep over them. Byron and Army were still watching from the main barn. He sent them a reassuring wave of his arm.

"Oh, look," Rory touched his arm and whispered, then pointed to a nearby tree. "Isn't that a beautiful bluebird? They usually aren't out in the fall. That's a sign of good luck."

Navy followed the line of her arm, and his eyes narrowed on the small bird. The bird cocked its head.

Before Rory saw his movement, a gunshot deafened her and the bird exploded with a bright flash of white. The next second she realized Navy was holding the weapon, still outstretched in his right hand. Her heart racing in terror, she stared agape at him.

"What did you—why did you—why do you have a gun?" she stuttered out, and began to back away from him.

Navy's expression, his body, his whole being seemed like a different man than the one who'd just made her mind spin with a kiss. His eyes were hard, his body tensed for response.

"That wasn't a bird," he bit out as he grabbed her arm and dragged her toward Byron and Army. When she struggled and stumbled, he practically lifted her feet off the ground with his pace.

"Let me go! What are you doing? Why did you kill that poor bird?"

"Rory, birds don't have hydrofuel cell batteries. Did you see that flash? That bird is a drone." He glanced down as he marched her ahead. "Your wolf is probably one, too."

"Are you insane?" she cried, feeling hysterical laughter bubbling up inside. Looking back at her father, she observed that the internal struggle evident in his expression seemed out of balance with the fact that an armed madman was dragging his daughter toward him.

Reaching the barn, Navy pulled Rory to a stop.

"Byron, it's time to go. You knew this day might arrive."

Byron shook his head slowly. "How do I know I can trust you?"

Rory's jaw dropped. "What? You can't trust him, Dad. Did you see that gun?"

Navy's eyes narrowed. "How much else doesn't she know?"

"It kept her safe."

Rory yanked her arm from Navy's grasp and stepped toward her father. She eyed Navy with obvious disgust and fear. He held her gaze but his tone was strictly business, and he seemed every bit the frightening soldier that others feared on sight.

"Not anymore. The cat's out of the bag. In fact, it's more like a lion on the hunt. Drones don't come in cute bluebird clothing without government funding." Looking to Byron, he said, "You tell her or I will. This is for her safety. The Resistance sent us to protect you both from TEAR."

"Who is the Resistance?" Rory hissed. "Didn't Mom *work* for TEAR?"

Byron sighed, his glance flicking from Navy to Rory. "How much time do we have?"

Navy glanced over his shoulder, scanning the trees, then to Army. "Is there anything we can do to buy time?"

His powerful forearms crossed over his broad chest, but his shrug was relaxed. "If we stay inside, we could throw up a jammer and prevent transmissions for a while, to a limited radius. After that storm, drones could believably be downed. We need to be out by tonight."

"What is everyone talking about?" Rory finally demanded. Looking to each face, she landed on her father's and saw at last a reassuring, if sad, expression. He took her hand and squeezed it briefly.

"You're soaked, sweetheart. Let's get indoors and talk."

"No. Now. Someone tell me what the fuck is going on." Her distrust and fright was quickly solidifying into a bone-deep rage at feeling like a helpless child talked over by condescending adults. Each of the men staring at her had the arrogance to presume her ignorance was protective, and she was not a fan of being ignorant or protected.

When Navy stepped toward her, she backed away. "I'm not going anywhere with you!"

Navy practically growled, "Rory, get inside the house now. You're entitled to an explanation, but not when every bug and bird out here could be listening."

Jaw clenched so hard her teeth ached, she stalked toward the house. She tore into her bedroom and changed out of rain-soaked clothes, and despite the weather still hovering in the eighties, her teeth chattered. The bird exploded in her mind repeatedly, and the white phosphorescent flash it made when he killed it so heartlessly seemed undeniably unnatural.

When she stormed back down the stairs, she heard their voices low in the kitchen: Navy and Army discussing signal blocking.

"I'm setting up my signal jammer and trying to amplify it using the solar panel system. I may get a broader reach, but if their systems are better than ours, we're still screwed," Army said. "I'm telling you, we need to move fast. I think in two camps."

Navy was nodding. "Rory comes with me, you take Byron. Get to the—"

"Quit talking about me like you get to choose where I go," she interrupted quietly from the doorway. She glared at Navy, as angry at herself for falling naively for a stranger as she was at him for deceiving her.

Navy lifted his head and took her in—a tall, slender, capable young woman who knew both far more than she probably realized, and far less than she deserved to understand. No matter how capable she was, she was not prepared for the danger ahead. But at this moment, she was also not prepared to give him even an inch of her trust.

Furious with himself for frightening her, yet certain it was necessary, he turned his anger on Byron.

"If you wanted your daughter to be capable, maybe you should have given her a goddamned clue how to protect herself."

"Don't talk to him that way!" Rory snapped, just as Byron said, "She knows how to defend herself."

"The sight of a gun left her shaking," Navy barked.

"The sight of a gun in the hands of a man she thought she knew."

"Stop talking about me in the damned third person!"

Abruptly, Army pulled a chair out for her. "Rory, why don't you sit down. I'll get you a drink, and these two can stop blaming each other for being protective of you. Beer or water?"

"Beer."

He cracked her open a bottle, set it down on the table as she took a seat, and spun another chair around to straddle it facing her. On the table she saw the remains of two more bluebirds, now cracked open with more surgical precision than Navy's bullets. She could see their mechanical innards, functional little computers with wings. Byron took a beer out as well and sat across the table from her. Navy stayed leaning against a counter, arms crossed.

After an uncertain silence, Army cleared his throat and said, "Let me kick this off. Rory, you might be the primary target of a government plot to solve the die-off by finding the most effective immune systems in the country and replicating them for the highest bidder."

CHAPTER 6

Byron took another drink of his beer but found the taste like sawdust on his tongue. He set it aside and met Rory's blue-green eyes.

"Your mother was obsessed with protecting you from infection. Whether the treatments she was developing worked or not, you got them. You had gotten adjusted to . . . I don't know . . . three shots a week by the time you were seven. We knew it couldn't hurt you to be exposed to the antibodies. She gave you donor antibodies and recombinant antibodies they were testing officially in their research labs. After age seven, it was evident that her research was failing. But . . . as you grew up, nothing ever fazed your immune system. We started to suspect there was something special going on with you before we moved from Boston."

"Is that why we moved?" Rory remembered that time. Memories tinged with urgency and relief: her mother suddenly working less and able to spend more time with her. Her father almost giddy to be in control of his surroundings.

"Partly. And for all the same reasons we told you. But when she realized that, despite all her years of research, you were the only experiment that succeeded, she was also beginning to suspect that the Task Force for Epidemiology and Antimicrobial Research was never planning to release a cure to the world. They were going to market it, commercialize it, control the world with it. And probably weaponize the diseases for which only they held the cure."

Rory shook her head. "And you're telling me no amount of research has found any antibodies that work?"

Byron sighed and shrugged helplessly. "Before Persy . . . Before she died, I was in the loop. She disengaged from almost everything related to the task force, and any minor research she did here was to, frankly, try to figure out why your immune system was so magical. But still, she traveled back to Boston infrequently to stay informed, consult for TEAR, just hoping she could pick up a clue. This pandemic isn't going to end, and having her daughter be the pawn in a worldwide battle to find a cure was unthinkable."

Rory shook her head and leaned over the table. "If I'm so magical, why am I at risk? Why wouldn't I just give my blood or stem cells to the research labs and let them solve this?"

Navy remarked, "And you're worried about trusting me?"

Her gaze snapped to him. "Yes. I am."

"What do you think they would do if you raised your hand and said, 'I seem to be the cure?'" Navy asked her. Her answer came without hesitation.

"Identify the useful antibodies, test them in vitro and then in vivo, create a recombinant version through a stem-cell line, and mass-produce them for humanity." She raised an eyebrow in challenge.

Navy came closer to her. "TEAR is run by a cabal of survivors who live in terror of dying as painfully and miserably as one-seventh of the nation already has. So far, every survivor they've asked to volunteer has never been seen by their families again. Your database, if they discovered it, could put thousands more families at risk. If they find you, they find the database. And they'll torture you to get any details they want. Once those details are available, you'll only be useful to them—in a coma," he added as he leaned an arm on the back of his chair and brought his face close to hers, "until you die." He held her eyes and watched the anger slowly recede, replaced as he had hoped by a dawning awareness of her situation. Shifting to a crouch beside her chair so their eyes were level, Navy softened his tone. "We aren't here to ruin your life. We're here to extend it. You need to trust us, and you need to leave."

Despite her determination to keep a mental distance from Navy, she found his nearness still made every nerve ending alert.

Meeting his frighteningly focused eyes, she took a short breath. "And go where? This is our home."

"It can't be anymore. We have a base; we'll take you there, and our scientists can work with you to try to develop a treatment—from whatever it is your body has learned."

Army said reassuringly, "A cure for everyone."

Rory looked to Byron, whose decision clearly was already made, but who also seemed resolved to follow her wishes. Her expression pleaded for guidance.

"Maybe, someday, we can come back here again. After you've made the world a better place. You have a gift, one that you didn't ask for or even earn. Do you remember Keats' line about the Muses?" It was one of his favorite pieces of poetry.

She closed her eyes, frowned, and then spoke softly. "*But strength alone though of the Muses born, is like a fallen angel: trees uptorn . . .*'" She opened her eyes. "I can't remember the rest."

He completed it. "*Darkness, and worms, and shrouds, and sepulchres delight it; for it feeds upon the burrs, and thorns of life, forgetting the great end of poesy, that it should be a friend to soothe the cares, and lift the thoughts of man.*'"

"Poetry and music are no different gifts than science. Being gifted the way you are, it could do the damage of a fallen angel. Or it could lift the thoughts and soothe the cares of man." Byron covered her hand in his and squeezed it.

Rory clenched her jaw against tears. She'd always known that was a quote her father loved; until today she hadn't understood why. It hurt to know he'd been hiding something from her for so long, something that obviously pained him, too.

"Okay. Then we leave, after we let the neighbors know to care for the chickens and take the apples."

Navy shook his head. "We can't let them know. You need to disappear quietly."

Rory glared at him. "The chickens will die. The gardens will rot. The neighbors deserve what we have—everybody's struggling."

Army held up a hand over Navy's firm reply. "Wait. I have an idea. If you were to invite all the neighbors, right away, for a celebration of the harvest ... would they come?"

Rory looked to Byron, and they both nodded.

Army explained, "Do it. We'll throw a party, have a bonfire, alcohol—all the signs of staying right here and sleeping in tomorrow. We'll all sneak out under cover of darkness and be miles ahead tomorrow when it's realized. If you trust someone well enough, you can let them know that they can take everything in a few days."

Navy slowly nodded. "It could work. It could work well. Let's start packing while they call everyone in."

CHAPTER 7

A bonfire roared with festive warmth as neighbors mingled in the twilight, laughing and catching up, enjoying the alcohol brought up from the Stevigson cellars. Last year's apple cider was keeping everyone warmer than the fire, and a makeshift rotisserie propped over a low area of the fire held a variety of meats and vegetables slowly roasting. Rory stood away from the crowd, committing everything she loved so dearly to a photo in her mind. It felt like an impossibility that she would never see this place again, and yet the future was no clearer than the now.

When she sensed him behind her, she let out a sigh.

Navy stood watching her: the long plait she'd put her hair into, the proud posture drooping in sadness. The warmth and light in her demeanor dimmed.

"Am I interrupting?"

"Yes."

Navy stepped forward. His voice was deep when he said, "You need to trust me, Rory. We've got a long road ahead, and we're bound together." He could practically see her hackles rise, but she wouldn't look at him.

"Everything you've told me before noon today is a lie. Don't tell me who I need to trust."

He took her by the elbows and forced her to look him in the eye. "No lies. Just omissions." Her eyes searched his face, and the cerulean eyes that had sparkled with laughter and intimacy hours ago were now like glaciers. Like all the other people who saw his face and looked away in distaste.

Icicles dripped from her voice. "Forgive me if I don't have the energy to parse your deceptions from truth."

"What happened between us was real, and you know it, even if you're angry about it." With a slow breath, he shook her gently. "Would it help if I said I'm sorry?"

She considered that. "No. You wouldn't mean it, and I wouldn't believe it."

Reluctantly, he let her go, fingertips traversing her forearms and hands. A farewell to the hope of touching her again. She had given him a taste of the warmth she could offer, and it had been addictive. But if cool distance was what she wanted from him, it was certainly his area of expertise.

"We'll leave at eleven," he remarked evenly. "I've packed you a bag, but there's room for more, only what you need most. We're taking the Jeep, but we may have to go on foot, too, and Army's taking the boat with Byron."

"Boat? Where is this base?"

"Fifty miles off the coast of Nova Scotia."

"So the Jeep will take us to . . . ?"

He shrugged, staring ahead. "Whatever boat we can find to steal and get us there." He ignored her pointed look at him and commented, "There's a woman running up behind us. Do I need to be worried?"

Turning, Rory saw the oncoming attack and grinned. She left him, and he turned to watch her embrace a young woman about her age who was even taller than Rory. They hugged tightly, Rory reluctant to release her. They leaned back and grinned at each other, obviously reuniting after a longer absence.

"Birdy, it's good to see you! I'm so glad you came!"

The taller woman laughed, a beautiful trilling sound that made even Navy fight back a smile. "Why wouldn't I?" Rory's friend was a uniquely beautiful young woman: rangy, strong but feminine, with striking cheekbones dusted by freckles and twinkling cornflower-blue eyes. Curling brown hair was haphazardly tied back, but ringlets escaped around her temples.

"Well . . . you've just been busy, I know. Let's go have a drink and catch up."

Birdy agreed but looked to Navy curiously. "Okay . . . but who's your friend?"

Rory looked to him, hesitant. His eyebrow barely lifted in challenge. She had to play polite here.

"This is Navy. He was traveling through with another friend from the military, and he was right in time to help us with the harvest. Navy, this is my oldest friend, Avis James. We call her Birdy."

Birdy let out another adorable guffaw. "No, we don't. Not since I was twelve. Hi, Navy. You can call me AJ." She extended an elegant hand, but when he shook it he could feel the calluses of hard work on her palm. "Nice to meet you." Perceptive eyes took in his dark-lined visage, but her height was almost matched to his and she showed no intimidation.

"Nice to meet you, AJ." Yet another person who simply examined his face, then accepted him without question.

Smiling at her friend, Rory clapped her on the shoulder as she said, "Birdy and I have been friends since we were eight. She's the best fisherwoman in Massachusetts—" but she halted when AJ winced at the contact and folded her body away in pain.

"Sorry, Rory. I got nailed there with a hook when we crossed lines with another trawler. Idiot cut the line under pressure and . . ." she whistled a sound of something flying through the air, "bam, right in my shoulder. Had to pop it through, cut the barb to get it out."

Rory's brows furrowed with concern. "I'm sorry, Birdy. Is it infected?"

"I hope not, but it's kind of hard to see."

"Let me look." Rory stood behind her, and AJ pointed to the spot so she could tug down the back of AJ's shirt. A slim bandage did a poor job of covering the swollen, red patch of skin that had streaks of darker red radiating out from it. Rory looked up at Navy and gave a short shake of her head. She tried to hide the fear in her voice when she said, "Let's go inside and put something on this. C'mon."

Inside the house, Rory took AJ and Navy to the basement under the guise that their first aid kit was stored there. But once they were belowground, she headed to another door and paused at the handle.

"Birdy, we've been friends for almost our whole lives. What I'm about to show you—it can't be shared with anyone, okay?" Rory began. AJ looked from her friend to Navy, who seemed unperturbed by the impending revelation. Actually, his demeanor seemed to AJ to be unflappable at any junction.

"This is for Rory's safety," Navy said to her, sensing that she needed a reason not to be alarmed. AJ nodded.

"Okay . . ."

The door opened, and the dirty brick walls of the basement turned into clean white laminate and stainless steel, a small room with lab equipment and a single lab bench in the center, clean of any evidence of research. Though Byron and Rory had not told Navy about the lab, he'd suspected it was here or perhaps under the barn where he and Rory had sought shelter during the storm.

"You knew my mom was a researcher. This was her lab. I've used it some, too, but I'm nowhere near her level of expertise." Rory's humility was calming, taking the edge off of AJ's obvious anxiety. "But there may be something here that can help you. I need to let you in on something, though."

AJ eyed her warily. "Dude, you walk me into your secret basement science lair and tell me there's more secrets to share. You are starting to freak me out. Get to the damned point."

Rory smiled and gave silent thanks for her friend's unique sense of the absurd. "It appears while my mom's research wasn't successful, it was effective at making me very resistant to infections. And the research that has continued after she—died—" she tripped a little on the word, eyes dropping. "It hasn't made progress either. So, there are people looking for me now."

"Not good people." Navy took over for a second, holding AJ's gaze. "I'm here to protect Rory and Byron, and the best way to protect them is to get them to a safe location, quietly, and solve the science there."

AJ needed no help grasping his subtlety. "You're going to disappear them?" She looked to Rory, who nodded. "So my father's incessant paranoia about the government hiding a cure, that's for real?"

Rory bobbled her head. "Close. They want to sell a cure, once it's found, only to people who can afford an outrageous price tag."

AJ abruptly pointed to Navy's chest. "I don't know this guy from Adam. Why are we trusting him?"

Rory took a long breath. Her eyes held Navy's, and her next words felt to him like a scalpel slicing a quick, neat slice. "I'm not sure I am. But I have seen evidence that he's right, and that we're being watched. My dad knew that the government wasn't being honest about the real mission of Mom's research. That's why they moved here. So, we're leaving tonight and we'll be gone tomorrow. I won't be able to stay in contact without putting you at risk. But I hoped you would come back, take the chickens, take the apples and sell them for your family. And the gardens—anything you need."

Navy watched the dawning awareness on AJ's face that her friend was soon to vanish.

"This is crazy, Rory."

Rory nodded. "It is. And I hate it. But . . . I believe it's what I should do. Where we're going, I may be able to resume my mother's research. Maybe I can help prevent more deaths."

"So, if you do this, if you succeed, maybe I won't have to fear my brothers . . . my dad . . . my future kids . . . dying?"

Rory nodded. "I hope so."

Birdy's tough shell was an isinglass curtain to Rory. She knew the fear in her eyes was also about her own survival, about the heat likely starting to prickle painfully between her shoulder blades. Rory grabbed her hand and squeezed. "Do you trust me? Remember the fish-blood oath? If I'm right, you'll heal up in days. And though I'll be gone, you'll know then that I made the right decision. I promise I'll find a way to check in and ask you. Let me do this."

Birdy's glacier-blue eyes slowly sparkled, their old friendship fluent in far more than speech alone. She remembered the children's fable about a man trading blood with a fish, the one her father had told any children who would sit near his feet. Rory smiled, too.

"Let you do what?" Navy asked quietly.

Birdy raised her eyes to him, and he wondered how many people found her sheer power of confidence less than intimidating. "She's going to give me a blood transfusion."

CHAPTER 8

Navy's eyes whipped to Rory, who was already rummaging in drawers and withdrawing needles and telltale rubber tourniquets. "You've got to check something first, right? What about matching blood types?" There seemed a shortage of protocol in the process. Rory shook her head without looking to him.

"I already did. I'm type O neg. In fact, I'm type O neg neg, meaning I don't carry cytomegalovirus, which can infect people who are also not already exposed to it. So there's actually no one I'm not compatible with."

She was already tightening off the rubber cuff above her elbow, painting her skin with iodine wash, and unsheathing a needle. Looking up at him, she said, "Now is the time for all queasy souls to look away." He almost did, when she pressed the enormous-looking needle into her skin and it slid through, slicing under the surface like a seabird diving for a fish. The dark red welled into the needle's tube with the pressure of life wanting to grow, and she had only to let its force slowly depress the plunger for it to fill the fat syringe. "Good enough," she whispered to herself, and slid the needle out as she replaced it with a square of gauze. With swift, business-like efficiency, she taped her elbow to hold the gauze, capped the syringe, and shifted her attention to Birdy.

By the time Navy decided to leave the small lab, the needle from Rory's arm had already pierced the skin of AJ's. He was, despite his years in the military, feeling queasy. It was one thing to see men in his unit being treated. Watching Rory's blood fill a tube, though, caused acute anxiety. When he emerged on the porch, he found Byron rocking in a porch chair, making broken music with his harmonica.

"Hello, Navy. I see you've discovered our lair," he drawled ironically. He knew the creak of the basement's door. There was only one reason for Rory, Navy, and AJ to be missing, and that door to also creak.

Navy's answer was only a long breath in. Out.

"Something there you found distasteful? Shocking? Useful?" Byron let out a bitter laugh at the lack of response. "No? Me either." The harmonica whined a bluesy dirge.

"AJ has an infection." He didn't miss the sharp intake of Byron's breath against the harmonica's vocal chords. "Rory gave her a small transfusion."

Byron shook his head in dismay. "It took her hours to realize that she has a universally compatible blood type. It took us years to realize the risk of that." He looked up at Navy and stood from his chair to stand abreast. "Do you have a grasp now for why I kept her in the dark so long?"

Navy nodded. He almost felt his heels click together in deference and respect. His elbow itched to snap a salute.

Byron's body seemed almost to vibrate with fear and anger as he and Navy faced off. "Do you have a grasp of how precious she is? How desperately I need you to protect her?"

"We all need to." Navy's boot-camp hoorah seemed appropriate here, the sound of an individual submitting to the best interests of his team, but as the collective noun "we" left his mouth, he felt like a hypocrite and a liar. Byron knew it, too, and stepped so close he could smell his breath.

"Fuck everyone else. You don't think of her as a commodity, as a cure, do you?" Byron said barely above a whisper, but it felt like a roar to Navy.

"No," he said instantly. "I don't."

"I need to know you'll—"

"I *will* protect her."

Byron didn't need to hear Navy's words. The near violence in his eyes, the ferocity caged in his form, carried the note as clearly as air through Byron's harmonica. Byron nodded, and Navy matched it in response.

"Daddy? Everything okay?" Rory's voice came from behind them.

"How's my missing twin daughter? Did you guys finally make the fish-blood oath?" Byron almost hid the crack in his voice.

Rory smiled, and AJ appeared at her side, arm in arm. "Yeah." When she couldn't handle the gleam in his eyes, Rory looked from her father to Navy, ready to blame him.

"It's time to go," Navy said abruptly.

She visibly paled. "You said eleven."

"I changed my mind."

"We can't—"

"We can. Go pack. AJ can help you," Byron intervened. Rory read his face and nodded assent. She disappeared upstairs, and Byron's gaze met Navy's again. "I'm going to say goodbye to friends. Without saying goodbye. When I come back, you two will be gone and my daughter will be safer."

Navy nodded. "I swear to you, I'll keep her safe. You'll see her soon again."

When AJ left the house again, she started for the party of neighbors and friends, but her emotions were running too high not to arouse suspicion. She decided a short walk would clear the threatening tears, so she headed to the chicken coop to remind herself how many they had and what to do to care for them. The light off the corner of the house kept the coop lit and mostly deterred would-be assailants.

A man's tall form was crouched by the coop, a small set of tools on the ground beside his knee. Judging by his military-issue drab shirt and cargo pants, she wondered if this was the "military friend" of Navy's. His hair was shaved clean, his arms and back were heavily muscled, and AJ reminded herself that strolling up to strangers wasn't wise at any age. But she was intrigued, and she dealt with big men every day of her life.

"Hello."

He didn't flinch or turn, which led her to believe he had known she was walking up long before she saw him.

"Hello there," was his reply, in a warm and friendly voice that indicated he wasn't quite as tense as his darkly marked friend. She detected a Caribbean accent. "I'm Army. You must be AJ."

"Army? You must be Navy's pal?"

"Yup. Give me a second, I'm just installing something."

AJ crossed her arms and watched him. It looked like a tiny metal box, with short wires hanging off it. After a few adjustments, he locked it into place just under the coop's low-slung roof, pointed up and out, and then checked his wrist phone. Illuminated on his strong forearm appeared the video of them, revealing his face to her and vice versa. As if his arm were a mirror, their eyes met.

He grinned, and she thought her heart fluttered a little. She smiled a little, too, unable to resist the charm of his well-hewn face. Army stood and turned, and she smiled in amusement again.

"Sorry. I just don't often meet men—people—taller than me."

"I don't usually meet women nearly as tall as me." He extended a hand and AJ considered it, then shook it. She had a confident grip, he thought. Navy had told him what he knew about the only person who would stay tonight and know anything about their plans.

"I'm AJ. Or Birdy. Whatever."

He seemed to be studying her, seeing her saddened mood. She broke the silence with a gesture to the coop.

"So, you're installing cameras?"

"Yup. If you wear skirts when you come to check on the chickens, that won't bother me at all."

The joke caught her off guard and earned a peal of unexpected laughter that shot straight to Army's heart. It was like a bird's song.

"I usually prefer longer formal wear for cleaning up after chickens." She sighed, adding, "I just wanted to come remind myself of what to do. With the chickens, I mean."

Turning, he stood beside her and watched the birds peck lightly at the dirt.

"You know, it's okay to be upset by this. I know it was a bit of an ambush. I'm still worried Rory might punch me."

"She would." She sighed. "Thank you. I'm just scared for her, and worried I won't see her again."

"And worried for yourself?"

AJ passed him a reluctant, guilty glance. "My father is a bit of a conspiracy nut. If I believe him, men in black may come for me soon."

He turned to face her, then gently touched her arms and turned her to face him. "Listen, you don't know me from Adam. But I'm a Navy SEAL. I've been doing this for a while. And I want you to remember something: if anyone asks you anything about Rory, the way to keep her safe, and you safe, is to tell them absolutely everything you know. You don't have to write them a novel, but if they ask you a question, you give them the answer."

AJ, confused, shook her head.

Army smiled, his warm brown eyes holding hers. "They don't want what they already have. If you give them what they want, they will leave. And you don't know where we're headed, so you can't put her at risk that way."

PART TWO

Wild Nights

CHAPTER 9

Stevigson Farm, Woods Hole, Massachusetts

Rory climbed into the Jeep beside Navy, shutting the door quietly in the dark barn. With everyone distracted by the barbecue and her father's starting up a music circle, if she and Navy disappeared, the only assumptions would be of the sniggering sort.

"You ready?" he asked. He turned the key, and the electric-powered Jeep barely whispered when its engine lit.

"No," she said angrily. "But even if I had a year I wouldn't be ready."

He took her chin and turned her face to his. In the dark shadows of the barn, the colored swaths of his skin seemed to disappear. "You'll see this place again."

"I hope you mean that."

"You'll come to learn, Rory, that I mean everything I say." Turning back to the wheel, he shifted into drive and wheeled quietly out, with no headlights and heading north.

Washington, DC, TEAR Headquarters

An alert flashed across the holo-screen of the analyst working the late shift. He clicked it—another glitch, another reset in the nano-drones at the farm. His two coworkers were asleep at their own desks, but he'd become accustomed to this shift. And, as with all government agencies, it was run by idiots who had no idea how often he hacked into classified files. If the world wasn't so hopeless already, he would probably be able to sell some secrets for a life on a Greek isle—or more likely a Chinese one—but until someone found a new source of medicine, there wasn't anything very valuable here to be sold.

Not that he didn't have reason to hope. If this chick in Massachusetts was the gold mine they were suspecting, there might be an especially lucrative secret at his fingertips soon. Though her dead mother had been useless to help find the cure, everyone seemed to think *she* was the cure.

"She can be the cure for what ails me," his coworkers loved to sneer. And they were right, she was a hot piece of ass. But he could afford many, many hot pieces if she ended up being the secret the world needed to prevent human extinction. How, he wasn't sure. He knew they thought she was somehow knowledgeable of her mother's research, but he had reason to doubt. Hell, she was homeschooled. All he could tell she was decent at was computers and research. Boring.

Another alert flashed, and he tapped the touch pad. This one was an alert, not from a drone, but a vehicle tire plug. Transmitting movement from the farm, headed north. Seemed odd, but he didn't have the drones working right, so he hadn't been able to watch or listen for a few hours, resetting all their transmitters. That electrical storm had been vicious, but the analyst supposed it hadn't been able to affect the transmitters embedded into tires.

"Somebody out for a beer run?" he mused. Shifting to a second holo-screen, he tapped a drone that was on the outskirts of the farm, expecting another transmitter fried by the storm. But this one lit up the screen in perfect detail, the road into the farm from the north. The vehicle hadn't passed this drone yet, so he switched to another drone on the south perimeter.

Perfect transmission.

He tried others, sometimes with success, sometimes failure, till a pattern emerged. If he drew a map from the center of the house, signals were blocked in all directions at roughly equal distances. Surely the storm hadn't created failures in such a symmetrical pattern. He went back to the exit road and waited. The family Jeep drove by, windows up, too dark to see driver or passenger. Just a hint of both.

"Odd." But was it worth alerting higher command? He decided to track them for an hour or less. A run to get beer shouldn't be a long one.

CHAPTER 10

Docks near Stevigson Farm, Woods Hole,
Massachusetts

At eleven, as they had planned, Byron and Army boarded the small boat Byron had owned for years. After the engine had failed almost three years earlier, he hadn't quite found the motivation to get it fixed. It was reassuring, as Byron quietly shoved off the dock guided solely by the light of a sliver moon in a cloudless sky, to know that Army had repaired it in a day. His mechanical skills seemed to come naturally, as he had already assured Byron that he'd checked both the Jeep and the boat for any bugs or tracking devices shortly after their plan to sneak away was hatched.

"How long, how closely, have we been watched?"

"Hard to say, but the drones I caught were carrying cameras with high resolution and low zoom function. Not low-tech by any standard, but not the best available to the military. Meaning unless they were in your face, they were probably not able to hear many conversations. And we turned all phones and communication tools off. That's the only way to be sure no one's listening."

Byron nodded in the dark, eyes focused on the water and the coordinates Army had given him. He glanced at his copilot and was still unnerved and fascinated by the greenish underlight of his skin where the moon touched it.

"Do you think they'll be followed?"

"I hope not." Army could only shrug. Byron's nervous breath in and out reminded him that, for possibly the first time, he'd entrusted his daughter's whereabouts and safety to a man he hardly knew. Army had never known a friend as loyal, a soldier as fearless, or a person with as much integrity as Navy. But to Byron, he barely qualified as an acquaintance.

Reaching over, he clasped Byron's tall shoulder.

"There is no one she'd be safer with."

Byron returned his focus to the inky horizon, but his chest was tight with the knowledge that, for probably two weeks, he would have no idea if Army was right.

CHAPTER 11

Near the New Hampshire-Maine State Line

Navy glanced over at Rory, who had finally given in to sleep around four a.m. Curled on her side in the reclined seat, she looked peaceful and frighteningly delicate. He knew she was strong, and he believed she could handle whatever happened. But he wished badly that he could shelter her from anything more jarring than yesterday's revelations. Now that the sun was creeping over the horizon, burning off fog, the sense of anonymity he had felt in the night was also evaporating.

If drones had been at the farm, their signal jamming theoretically would have prevented the drones from knowing to follow the Jeep. But he knew the jammer had its limits, and drones had none.

With that in mind, he adjusted the left-hand rearview mirror with its digital controls, tipping the mirror as horizontal as it could go to view the sky above them. It was almost light enough now to make out any drones close enough to follow. He cursed as his eyes discerned the form of a bird flying steadily behind and above them with an unwavering flight path. And an unnatural wingspan.

Just the sound of his whispered expletive woke her, and she straightened abruptly.

"What? What's . . . what's going on?"

He looked over at her, her eyes foggy with sleep. He longed to run a hand down her cheek in reassurance, but he knew it would be unwelcome.

"We're being followed."

She looked behind them at the flat expanse of empty highway

and turned forward in time to see a sign indicating they were nearing Maine.

"Use the side mirror."

Rory looked, bewildered, to the side mirror and saw it was tilted wildly forward. But then a form in the sky became clear, and eerie silence filled the car as the implications hit her. It never flapped its wings, never circled or even dipped. As steady as a jet plane, and terrifyingly close.

"So what now?" she whispered.

"It means one of two things. Either Army missed a tracking device, or this guy saw us leaving and was outside the range of the jammer."

"Or both." She touched her mouth. "But it's not terribly crazy that we might drive the Jeep somewhere. Take a trip."

"Yep. Until they realize that nobody's at the farm. And that it's just you and me, almost to Canada," Navy reasoned. "And that the boat is gone." She nodded, processing.

"Is there anywhere we can drive that he can't foll—"

"No."

"Can we shoot him, too?"

"Unwise." Navy snorted. "Not that I don't want to."

Rory said aloud, more to explain to herself, "As soon as he goes offline, they'll know why. And send more. And if there's a tracking device, we need to ditch it or ditch the Jeep, too."

Navy tapped his fingers on the wheel. "Know any big covered bridges or tunnels around here?"

"Why ask me? I thought you grew up in Maine. Or was that just a lie?"

Navy frowned. "I lived further north. This is closer to Boston, so I assumed you might have visited." He sighed, then added, "I told you, I haven't lied to you."

Rory's eyes lit. "Wait, I do know a covered bridge. Yes. I do."

Washington, DC, TEAR Headquarters

The analyst and his coworkers were now all awake. Just when he had woken them for help, the drones at the farm had come back online, showing a few partiers still drunk around a dying bonfire that must have been set up for a celebration while the drones were down.

One drone was on the path of the Jeep, already nearly to Maine, but no one had a gut feeling for why they were anxious. Something was just . . . off.

"It's probably just her going on a jaunt with that guy. That farmhand they hired."

"Yeah, maybe. I'm alerting the team, though. Commander Jacobs should be informed," said the lead.

They nodded in agreement and left him to the job. He dialed the commander on a secure line, connected after three buzzes. He gave him a quick briefing on the night's events, explaining the electrical storm and its possible connection to the downed drones.

"So they're near Maine? Could be a lovers' getaway?"

"Yep."

"Do you have a snapshot of the farmhand you think she's with, face-on?"

"Enh. Maybe a bad one, yeah. He's got some sort of . . . disfigurement or tattoo. No clue why she's into him. She's pretty hot."

"Whatever," Jacobs blew him off. "Just send me the damn photo."

Orders acknowledged, the analyst hung up and slid back to his primary station to search up a face capture. As he did, he noted the drone in Maine indicating a forty-five-degree turn in direction to the northwest, but he returned his focus to the old videos.

Windham, Maine

Rory pointed ahead to the bridge, an old wood-covered structure spanning a river and still, miraculously, open to smaller cars. Navy judged its total length at about thirty yards and slowed as they entered it, stopping about two-thirds into its length. The sound of the tires rumbling across the old boards echoed like a drumroll slowing to a nerve-wracking stop. He pulled his weapon from a side pocket of his pants and chambered a round.

He turned to her. "Whatever happens, act surprised."

"Why?" Rory's heart was beating faster, her breath short.

"Because if they think you don't know anything, you're safer."

With that frightening suggestion of interrogation, he got out of the Jeep and eyed the entrance to the bridge. Within moments, the huge bird wafted into the front of the bridge, its eight-foot wingspan flapping twice and sending a concussion of air Rory could actually feel lift the strands of hair at her temples. Talons that were clearly metal tapped at the wood boards. It folded up its wings and stared at them, towering at least four or five feet tall.

"Holy shit! That thing is huge!" she said, looking from it to Navy. He was leaning over the rail, pretending to admire the river and not to have seen it. "Look at that!"

She heard the gunshot before she saw his weapon, as he had fired under his left arm. She looked back at the bird in genuine shock to see half of its head blown off, sparking and wires exposed.

He walked toward it, releasing bullets into it, as the bird's chest opened like a nightmare cuckoo clock and a tube emerged, firing something toward Navy that struck the Jeep's rear corner. Navy fell at the same second.

Washington, DC, TEAR Headquarters

Commander Jacobs' secure phone rang, and he answered quickly.

"General Kessler. Did you get my email?"

"Who sent you that photo?" Kessler barked.

"Our analysts watching the Stevigson Farm, sir."

"When was it taken?"

Commander Jacobs scrambled back to his email to open and reread the data.

"Ah . . . three days ago."

"I need boots on the ground in Woods Hole now, Commander. Send in a tactical team and take the girl, by force if necessary. Just *don't harm her*," he emphasized. "I want your top retrieval team in there. I don't care about anyone else."

"Yes, sir. Sir, how do you know this man? The one with the tattoos on his face?"

Kessler was silent for a moment, then answered grimly, "We trained him. I thought we'd killed him."

CHAPTER 12

Windham, Maine

"Navy! No!" she screamed when he spun backward and fell to his side, the bird advancing on him. He was holding his left side with one hand, blood staining his shirt. Still he held out the weapon in his right, the gunshots deafening her as he fired again and again until the bird stopped moving and fell backward. Rory ran to him, diving to her knees.

"Oh, my God! Are you okay?" she asked as he collapsed onto his back. The wound was on the edge of his waist, but she couldn't tell exactly where or how severe.

"Yeah, I think." He hissed out a breath of pain and sucked in another through clenched teeth. "I think it grazed me." He let her carefully pull away the shirt and find the ragged but shallow wound oozing blood, and then she abruptly pulled her own shirt over her head and folded it up. She wore a tank underneath, and he watched her gently lay her shirt over his wound. He grunted in pain when she slowly applied pressure; then he relaxed as she ran to the Jeep and back with a suitable binding that could hold the makeshift bandage on.

Her blue eyes met his, a little panicked, but calm beneath. They both nodded in understanding. They had to get moving.

"You stay here, I'll check the Jeep for damage. We need a hospital or a clinic or something."

Navy pointed to the bird. "Cover its face. I just want to be sure it's not still relaying anything."

Rory looked over to it and then glanced behind her at the

bridge exit. He couldn't see her as she sprinted away, but when she returned it was with a stone the size of a volleyball. She walked past him to the bird, then viciously slammed the rock on its damaged head. Then she did it again. On the third time, he managed a laugh.

"Rory. It's done."

With a huff she straightened, then kicked it for good measure.

Rory first checked where the bird had fired into the Jeep and saw some minor damage to the inside wheelbase. Starting it again, she gingerly drove forward, testing its control. It was still running, though her instincts were that it wouldn't get them far past Maine. Hopping out again, she took the time to examine every wheel just in case. As she was about to head back to help Navy to the vehicle, a bit of debris on one wheel caught her eye.

Buried in the outer edge of the tire was a little nail. No, as she looked closer, it was a plug with a tiny wire hanging out. The end of the wire was slightly more bulbous. An antenna?

Running back to Navy, she helped him up as she explained the plug.

"So the correct answer was *both*. Can you pull it out?" He grunted again as she got him into the passenger side, his legs still on the ground as she squatted at the tire in question. He had to smile when, as he grabbed for his knife to suggest she pry it out, Rory reached behind her back and popped out a folding knife of her own. The transmitter was no larger than a grain of rice and hadn't even pierced into the tire.

"The river?" she suggested. Navy was considering their options when they heard a car ahead.

"Can you drag the bird behind the Jeep?" he asked urgently. She ran over, grabbed its feet, and tugged it over to the wall of the bridge nearest the vehicle. For all its ferocity, it was surprisingly light. She reckoned that was why Navy was still alive.

Rory looked at him and cocked an eyebrow at the frightening appearance he would give to a stranger. "Get in the car, shut the door. I got this."

His dark eyebrows dove. "What are you going to do?"

"I got this. Be quiet and look sullen."

"Rory. You don't have the skills for deception."

Rory's brows rose in challenge. "I have skills, Navy. Watch this."

Reluctantly, he got into the Jeep and closed the door.

As the car crested the hill ahead, they saw it was a truck, older and dirty and probably belonging to a local farm. She waited till it could see her, then pretended to be having trouble getting cell reception on her wristlet phone. The truck, driven by a young man, slowed as he took her in with a growing smile. She smiled back and waved at him, then leaned into his passenger window when he stopped.

A few seconds of conversation later, with some pointing down the road and a burst of flirty laughter that made Navy turn in his seat then almost cry in pain at the movement, and Rory hopped into the Jeep's driver seat to watch the truck disappear in their rearview mirror.

"He's headed all the way to Boston. To see his girlfriend. With TEAR on his tail."

Navy eyed her. "Does he know that?"

"Nope." She pulled away from the bridge, heading north again. "It's rolling under his passenger seat right now."

Navy gave her an admiring glance. "Where did you learn those skills?"

"Those skills were fired in the dark crucible of middle school, Navy."

A few miles down the road, they crested a hill into an area that Rory remembered visiting in her youth. It wasn't a vivid memory, but it involved a red-bricked hospital overlooking a small town. It didn't take long to find, and it was definitely not functioning.

"I guess my mother did research here . . ." she mused as she pulled up to the hospital's front entrance. A beautiful building at one point, but now shuttered, it showed signs of neglect.

"Maybe this is best. No one's here, so there's no record we're here. Let's just get in, get what we need, and get out," Navy suggested. "Surely there's some leftover first aid kits or bandages inside."

She looked over at him, wishing for more supplies—saline, antiseptic, probably a suture kit, too—then back at the building. He was right. There might be all those supplies inside, useless to anyone but them. Many hospitals had closed down after the die-off, resources exhausted, finances wiped, their community of customers beyond help. When antibiotics stopped working, even their most heroic efforts were in vain. And they'd walked away, what few employees remained to care. *How many ways did we do this to ourselves?* she heard her father saying in her head.

"Breaking and entering aren't among my skills. Do we just smash a window?"

Navy shrugged. "I'll knock first."

Getting inside wasn't as hard as she expected, after they found a back entrance with a digital keypad long disconnected from electricity. Once in, they were able to discern that they'd entered near the hospital's receiving bay for shipments and storage. Navy followed his instincts to the offices in the space and found an emergency supplies cabinet.

"Blizzards require flashlights. Growing up, we had one in every cabinet."

"Oh, so you weren't lying about growing up in Maine?" Rory mused.

"Dammit, Rory. I took a bullet for you. Call your dad a liar."

Rory shrugged. "Fair point. Sorry." A breath passed. "I believe the bird was aiming for *you*, though, so . . ."

Navy paused in his search and turned to glare at her. She held up her hands.

"Just to be factual."

He palmed his way through the cabinet and found two small flashlights, cheap but thankfully with batteries that were still taped at their ends to prevent energy loss. They set off through the maze of hallways and began a search of each area likely to have what they needed. "It's like a frozen slice of history," she whispered as their lights illuminated offices left with coffee cups still on the tables, and patient rooms cleaned, tidy, awaiting the next admission. The hospital had clearly been abandoned, probably without much warning by the look of it.

"The chapter of history where the healthcare system worked?"

She glanced over at Navy, who looked distinctly uncomfortable and angry. She wondered if this place surfaced memories of the treatment that had nearly killed him and marked him with the deep blue scars just below his skin.

"Well, some hospitals are still trying. Actually, I think the healthcare system was just one factor. Ruining antibiotics was a worldwide accomplishment." Then she sighed. "But yes, it feels like a photo of a time that was more hopeful." Navy looked at her and pointed his flashlight at a wall sign that gave directions before an intersection of halls: LABORATORY, ER.

In the laboratory Rory found gauze and bandages, supplies for various tests, but no antiseptic or even saline to wash the wound. Exploring on toward the ER, they found a supply cart still stocked with sterile bandages, gauze, needles, antiseptic scrubs and iodine paint, as well as sutures.

"Jackpot," she said. "Let's find a room with an exterior window so I can see better."

As they moved down the hall, a noise somewhere ahead of them froze their steps. Navy put a hand out to restrain her, just as a dark figure appeared at the end of the hallway. It looked male, wiry and leaning on a cane as it took them in.

"Who are you and what are you doing in my hospital?" the man rasped, in a voice deep and scratchy with age or infirmity.

"We're only looking for some supplies. We'll be gone soon," Navy said evenly. The man kept walking slowly forward, into the weak reach of their torches, and with each step forward Rory became a little more horrified by what she saw.

He was dressed in scrubs and a white lab coat, but the coat was stained with rusty brown splotches. His face was oddly disfigured, one side swollen with what seemed to be infected skin lesions, the other sunken with malnutrition. Thinning, scraggly hair was patchy on his skull. Evidence of many small surgeries riddled what skin showed, as if he'd been self-lancing and draining pustules in a vain attempt to keep himself alive. His sallow skin and eyes were jaundiced, but the kind of intense orange that she knew to be associated with certain classes of antibiotics.

He stopped a few feet from them. The smell of him nearly made her turn her head: a mix of body odor, antiseptic wash, and the battlefield putrescence of gangrene. Between them, Navy covered her hand with his.

"You're injured," the man in the lab coat observed, a gravelly growl.

"We just want—" Navy began.

"You can't have any medicines!" he suddenly screamed, and Rory jumped a little at the unhinged furor of his reaction. His teeth were stained green. "All the antibiotics here are *mine!*"

Navy squeezed her hand that he was holding, asking her to wait for him to answer, but she couldn't.

"Antibiotics are useless. Why would we want antibiotics?" she whispered, mystified. Almost glowing orange, his eyes pinned to her face.

"Some work. Work for a little bit—enough to sustain!" he screeched, and lifted his cane to gesture at her, his lips pulled back in a sneer.

"So you're just . . . you're just creating more resistance? You're probably a walking cesspool of resistant strains," she said almost to herself. The orange eyes were likely from rifamycin antibiotics, the jaundice from overuse, too. The green teeth indicated tetracyclines, another antibiotic with colorful side effects.

She was staring so intently at his mouth, Rory didn't realize he was advancing on her with his cane. He was already nearly touching her chest when Navy grabbed and yanked the cane from him. The man held on, stumbling toward Navy. Rory saw the man's left arm draw from his lab coat pocket, fist clutching a shiny object.

"Navy, he's holding something—" she started to shout, too late.

The ruse evaporated, the man dropping the cane and lunging with shocking strength at Navy. He was wielding an unsheathed syringe that he plunged into Navy's neck with a horrific scream.

The needle connected with the force of the man's stab, but by the time he'd struck his target, he was already being knocked unconscious, the cane now in Navy's hands whipped first under the man's chin with enough force to snap his head backward, then jabbed into his windpipe. The blow sent him flying backward. His head connected with a corner of a granite countertop, and he slumped to the floor.

Rory looked in shock to Navy, who was watching the man for signs of revival. The needle still stuck out of his neck.

"Jesus. What did he inject? Do you feel anything?" She examined the instrument, afraid to touch it and cause pain.

"I feel a needle in my neck, Rory," Navy said in fury. "Can you just take it out?"

She pulled it out, glad to see it was a small-gauge needle that would be unlikely to cause significant tissue damage. But who knew what had been in it? She turned to the man, her eyes narrowing on his lab coat. Crouching beside him, she hesitantly dug a hand into the pocket and pulled out two small containers: one generic centrifuge tube and a small medicine vial. Her light revealed its contents. She spun back to look at Navy.

"Navy, you need to find a place to lie down," she told him urgently, and he stood even as his legs began to falter. Guiding him to a bed down the hallway, she managed to ease him onto it and he leaned back, looked at her with glazing eyes.

"What was that?"

"Propofol. It's going to cause you to sleep."

"Take my gun," he said urgently. He could feel his brain relaxing, his senses dulling. She wouldn't be protected if he couldn't fight it. "Rory, look at me."

Rory leaned in, her hand on his shoulder. "It's okay, Navy."

"No, trust me, it's not. You're not safe. I can't protect you," he tried to say, but even the end of the sentence was hard to get out.

She rolled her eyes at him and then said with an optimist's tone, "I've had plenty of your protection. At least you won't be able to feel me stitching you up."

"Rory." His hand grasped hers and tightened on it. As he slipped into unconsciousness, she heard some honest thoughts that his conscious self probably wouldn't have said. "I take a bullet and a needle for you, and you roll your eyes at me?"

She let out a breath as his head dropped back, and she searched her memory for every fact she'd ever read about first aid, about propofol, about sedatives.

Heart rate. Blood pressure. Add fluids. She looked around, wishing for electricity so that she could see everything, use everything. *Not that I'd know how to work any equipment.*

Equipment. Wristlet. She wore a wristlet phone, and though Army had turned off its communication ability, it still had embedded in it an accelerometer, a heart rate monitor, and blood pressure sensors. Slapping hers onto his limp, heavy wrist, she activated the hologram screen onto his forearm and pulled up the health monitors. His heart rate was low, but not dangerous. Fifty-five beats per minute, holding steady for a full minute. His blood pressure seemed stable, if low. Now to hydrate him.

If saline was anywhere, she expected, it would be in a storage room here or in the lab. She hated leaving Navy's side, but she needed more supplies than she had. And, glancing at the man in the lab coat, she hated leaving him nearby that asshole. Grabbing the syringe and the bottle of propofol, she tipped it up and loaded the syringe again, then stabbed the bastard in the neck as hard as he'd done to Navy.

"And stay down, you sick bastard." Standing, she paused in thought. The other vial . . . what had it been? She held it up to the light, saw the tan-green drop of fluid still at its pointed base, and her stomach turned in fear. Opening its lid released its scent, confirming her suspicion.

He had injected Navy's carotid with a syringe full of propofol. And his own pus.

The propofol wore off a couple of hours later, giving Rory time to clean Navy's wound and place a few sutures that tied the jagged edges of his small wound closed. She learned in the process that she wasn't very squeamish, but also that it was far easier to stitch up a person whose pain couldn't register. She also learned that Navy's body, strong and lean and attractively muscled, had experienced the same discolored side effect as his face. The last swath of dark blue skin dipped under the waistband of his pants. She didn't look further.

An historical display discovered in her search for saline, food, and water had yielded the old-fashioned blood pressure cuff now circling Navy's upper arm. She had also found a room with an external window that helped her see him as he began to wake.

"Hey," she greeted when he was able to focus his dark amber-green eyes on her. "How do you feel?"

He first looked from her to the saline bag hanging from an IV.

"Salty. And hot. Did you turn on the electricity or something?"

Rory frowned. "No." Reaching out from her perch beside him on the stretcher, she laid a hand across his forehead. He was warm. She'd checked his temperature only fifteen minutes before. Now, twisting his wrist into her lap again, she activated the wristlet phone's display and read the metrics. Heart rate low. Temperature high. His blood pressure had dropped off.

"What's going on, Rory? Are you okay?"

Her blue-green eyes rose to his, and he read the worry in them. "Yeah, I'm fine. Tell me what else you feel."

He started to answer, then cringed and coughed abruptly for a few moments. He tried to sit up, shook his head, tried to stand, and then leaned back into the stretcher.

"Don't lie to me, Navy." It was a warning, but he could hear the fear.

"What did he inject me with, Rory? I feel like shit. I feel feverish, weak, sore all over." When dizziness darkened his vision, he let out a sharp curse and added, "We really need to keep moving."

She helped him back onto the stretcher. "I think he injected you with his own infection drainings." She took a deep breath and admitted to herself what she already knew. "And I think you're septic. If he hit your carotid, it would send the infection right into your bloodstream."

"Why do you sound like a doctor? How do you know all this?" He focused a blurring vision on her, and she saw how helpless he felt.

Rory shrugged and found herself running a hand down his face. She offered a joke. "I like to read?" Their gazes held, and Rory saw she didn't need to explain anything for him to understand what she was planning.

"No." It was an order.

"It's the only thing we've got."

"No, Rory."

"You don't need to be afraid. You get to take the fish-blood oath."

"I'm not afraid. I don't want you in danger. I want you to leave. Leave me here, take the Jeep, find a boat. I'll give you the coordinates—"

Rory shook her head. "I'm not leaving you, Navy. And I certainly don't know how to pilot a boat in the North Atlantic."

He struggled to sit up, but it felt like his blood was boiling under his skin. Navy's strength to fight left him, as did his grasp on time as she left his side, reappearing after what felt like an eternity. She had a metal table, a set of supplies he didn't understand.

This wasn't like the procedure with AJ. She didn't use a syringe, but instead a fat needle connected to a clear tube. As she sat on the bed next to him, the blood left her body and filled a transfusion bag.

"No, Rory," he kept trying to say. His tongue felt too heavy to lift.

After the bag seemed full to bursting with her blood, she clamped it closed and pulled the needle from her arm. Navy passed out.

CHAPTER 13

Washington, DC, TEAR Headquarters

The conference room vibrated with tension. Analysts cowered at one end of a conference table, terrified to meet the face of General Kessler seated opposite, flanked by Commander Jacobs and two of his reports.

"You had all fifteen drones working. You had them dart the vehicle with a tracker. You knew two visitors had arrived. All the drones stopped working, the vehicle went for a cross-country drive, their boat is gone, and the visitors disappeared. And now you tell me none of that seemed worthy to invoke a call until a day ago, and that you've completely lost their trail?"

"Well, they apparently found the dart and, I don't know, threw it into a passing truck," a junior analyst answered Kessler's scathing summary after a painful silence.

"They. And do we even know who *they* are?" Kessler barked.

"You seem to know better than we do. Better than, in fact, any facial recognition intelligence databases at our disposal." The senior analyst crossed his arms over his chest. "Who are *they*?"

CHAPTER 14

Windham, Maine

When Navy woke, the sun was cresting the horizon and lighting up the room they were in. He felt a pressure on his chest and looked down to see the blonde head of a sleeping Rory tucked under his bare shoulder. Her arm was wrapped protectively across his chest, and in the crook of her elbow a telltale bandage covered her veins. His own elbow bore a matching bandage.

He took measure of his own system. Neat stitches on his waist. Starving, but hydrated. Slightly weak, but well rested. Normal temp. Normal heart rate. A sore spot on his neck from the needle puncture. According to his watch, it had been about twenty-six hours since he was last fully conscious and feeling almost dead.

Was it possible for a blood transfusion to so completely reverse that? He knew far less than she did about this type of thing, but the sharp contrast was undeniable. A day before, he thought he was reliving the near-death experience that had left him broken, scarred, and terrified. Now he felt like he was getting over a cold.

He looked down at her, the dark blonde eyelashes casting shadows on her cheekbones, the soft pink lips and pale complexion. The skin under her eyes was smudged with fatigue. She must be exhausted, too. She'd probably had only a handful of hours of sleep in the past forty-eight. His gun was positioned inches from her hand on a metal stand, as if she'd wanted it ready to grasp and protect him with should someone find them. As if she knew how to use it. The thought of her trying, or needing to, sent a chill through him.

Navy knew she might not let him touch her again. She might

never really decide to trust him, especially considering what omissions were yet to be revealed. But at this moment, knowing that she had shared her life with him to save him, watched over him, and made sure he was whole again, he knew he couldn't stop trying. It was his job to protect her, but it was his personal mission to make her fully his to protect. He would do whatever it took to convince her, sacrifice whatever he needed to keep her safe.

Running a hand over her hair, he pressed a featherlight kiss to her forehead. The touch woke her, her eyes opening slowly before she fully awoke and bolted upright to look at him.

"Are you okay? Did you hear something?" Her head whipped around as she feared she'd fallen asleep and left them exposed. Rory looked back to Navy and saw he was giving her that intense stare she'd come to know, though it still fried her nerves. Now, though, it seemed tender, too. She felt herself blushing, realizing that he'd woken first, which meant he had found her curled up next to him when she had expected to be up and seated elsewhere when he came to.

"I'm more than okay. Thanks to you, it seems." He lifted his left arm slightly to bring attention to the bandage at his elbow.

She checked his temperature and heart rate, then scanned his face again. He wondered if she could feel his heart speed up at her fingers on him.

"Everything's back to normal."

"Not really," he replied, the corner of his mouth twitching up.

"It's not?"

"You saved my life. Thank you, Aurora Stevigson."

Rory took a shaky breath at the look in his eyes. "You're welcome," she whispered. Clearing her throat and looking away, she said, "You must be starving. I found some things in the cafeteria that were still edible."

"Yeah, actually. Ravished."

She pivoted off the bed and pulled around a tray table with a few cans of food and bags of chips, dried fruit, and nuts. He cocked an eyebrow.

"Not what you were craving?" she cracked.

"I'm having flashbacks to boot camp."

"Well, act grateful. It was really creepy to sneak past that guy." She gave a shiver. "I would've expected the propofol I gave him to wear off by now."

He frowned at her with apparent confusion. Thinking she needed to explain, she shrugged, "He deserved it. And I didn't want him to come to while I was stitching you up."

Navy swallowed. "Rory. He was dead from the moment I first hit him. I snapped his neck."

She blinked. "How . . . how do you know?"

"Because I was trained to do that."

Now she swallowed, hard. It hadn't occurred to Rory to ask him what his job really had been in the military. She had that sudden sensation, like back at the farm, that she didn't even know him. Yet she'd just fallen asleep on his chest.

He could see the goose bumps rise on her arms while she stared at him, processing. And he watched the trust slip a little farther away.

"I forgot to ask what you did in the military."

"I was a Navy SEAL. And I was trained to do that when I felt my teammates' lives were threatened."

Rory didn't say anything more, just nodded and turned away to look out the window.

"We need to get going soon. We need to ditch the Jeep." When she glanced back at him in surprise, he elaborated. "It's been over a day since their bird disappeared in the same location that their tracker reversed course and turned south. If that schmuck in the truck hasn't been pulled over by a team in black yet, he soon will be. That means they'll start the search again at the bridge, but this time with urgency."

"Because they know that we know."

"Yep. So if we can't find a replacement for the Jeep soon, it's going to be on foot."

Rory eyed the wind moving the trees. "It's cooler outside. I think there could be a storm blowing in. Are you sure you're able to hike any distance?"

"Any distance."

"You've been shot, stabbed, and infected."

"Poked, not stabbed. And the fact that your transfusion worked to stop my infection proves to me how badly we need to become invisible. Can I have your wristlet?" Rory tossed it to him. "It stays here. Before we leave, I'll turn on the cell signal. If you want to send Byron a message, that's fine, and it'll ensure they come here first. Just be vague on details."

"Won't they know where he is, then?"

Navy shook his head. "No, he won't receive it. Army turned off his com."

Rory turned back to the window, unexpectedly depressed to realize what should have been obvious. Navy wasn't giving her a chance to send her dad a message, or caring how she felt about her father, he was just conducting the mission. She should really stop reading anything into those intense moments between them. For him, Rory was an objective.

She jumped when Navy's hand unexpectedly slid down her arm and closed over her hand, and she looked up to him.

"Byron's going to be fine. Army's the only guy I'd ever want on a weeklong boat trip with me," he said reassuringly. "C'mon, let's get going."

CHAPTER 15

Five Miles off the North Atlantic Coast, North of Freeport, Maine

Byron poured two cups of coffee in the tiny galley of his ancient boat, stirred in a small spoonful of molasses he had indulged in bringing, and brought them aft to where Army was manning the helm. The sunrise was blinding on the horizon, and it lit the surface of the Atlantic Ocean with a dazzling sparkle.

Army thanked him and took a sip, then sent him a quizzical look.

"Molasses. Actually, sweet-potato molasses. I noticed you used sugar back at the farm."

Army chuckled and his accent seemed to thicken when he said, "You won't believe this, but my grandmama made something like that, back in Trinidad."

"Must have been a wise woman," Byron smiled.

"She was a firecrackah."

"You said Marines took you in when you were a boy. Why was that?" Byron probed.

"Everyone was dead. I was all alone," Army shrugged casually, but Byron's stomach clenched at the picture the few words painted. A young boy, orphaned by a plague of infections that had been killing off the population. "I was only eight. It was an act of mercy that they broke so many rules to protect me, but I guess you could say a band of brothers had pity for me. They brought me back to the states, to Florida, and one of the men adopted me. 'Bout broke his heart when I opted to join the Navy." They both chuckled to lighten the darkness of the story.

"What did you and Navy do . . . in the Navy?"

"We were SEALs. Strictly covert missions. Then, about three years in, they started to draft us into TEAR. We couldn't figure why. I mean, as far as we knew, TEAR was just a box of lab geeks trying to save the world with their microscopes." Casting a look askance at his boatmate, Army added wryly, "No offense."

"None taken. My wife would be proud of that epithet. And I'm a climatologist anyway."

Army continued, "General Kessler, the sort of silent commander of TEAR, convinced us that they needed us. That certain factions were holding survivors hidden from the world, or the survivors were scared and hiding, and they needed those survivors to progress their research. That seemed true for a few recovery missions."

Byron studied him, watching a sadness creep over his face. "But?"

"But. It was all a lie. We found ourselves taking children from their families. Parents from their kids. It was awful. We told them they'd get to come back soon." He let out a steely breath between his teeth. "I think I'll spend my whole life plotting how I can undo that. If they're still alive."

"They probably are, though perhaps in induced comas. Too valuable to lose. Discovering that was what made Persy leave TEAR, though no one knew she'd uncovered the truth. Even her fellow researchers probably don't know about that."

Army sighed. "I hope you're right. Navy and I still plan for a day when we can free them. Actually, that planning is exactly what got us turned into guinea pigs. Most of our team felt as we did, and we were developing a tactical plan. But other members of the select force, they felt forcing people to be donors was worth it for the greater good. I guess everyone feels differently about losing a loved one to the die-off. They made sure Kessler knew about it. So we and ten other men suddenly woke up on gurneys. Said the shots were to make us resistant, said they'd found the cure and we were the first people to get it as a reward for our service." Army grinned at Byron. "Imagine what a bunch of dumb young fucks we were, eh?"

Byron nodded. "We all have been at one point. I'm sorry you were taken advantage of. But I'm glad for my sake and my daughter's that you survived." They watched the ocean again in silence. Just as Byron was about to offer to make breakfast, one of the two fishing poles he'd positioned to trail off the stern began to spin its reel.

"Breakfast is knocking," Army said hopefully, throttling back to stop the boat. Byron worked the line, reeling in a sizable cod while Army applauded.

"I'll be damned. It's a cod!" Byron exclaimed as he freed it from the hook. He turned to set the line down in a safe spot and, as he turned back, jumped in shock as Army's arm crashed a wooden cosh on the fish's head, executing it with a single sharp blow.

"Jesus. I planned to put it in the live well."

Army barely glanced at him. "You do mean to eat it, right?"

"Well, yeah."

"Then he's better off now. It's cruel and unusual punishment to do that slow smother to a fish, Byron."

Byron gave it a moment's thought and decided he quite agreed with the younger man. Leaning back on his heels, he studied the fish respectfully. Army watched him staring at it in wonder.

"Ahh . . . I didn't mean you have to give it last rites."

Byron chuckled and then gave in to a long, deep belly laugh that felt very good in spite of the recent seventy-two hours of pure stress.

"I was just reflecting on history, Army." Standing up, he took the fish to the cleaning table built into the back edge of the stern and set to work on the process to make it edible. "This fish helped build America. They say they used to grow as big as men, the largest must have been as long as this boat. They say you used to scoop them out of the ocean with buckets. It kept Native Americans alive, then colonists. It was probably the most eaten fish in the Americas and Europe in the 1800s."

"So we overfished it?"

"Yep. Till it was practically extinct. Even this boat's nets helped. Oh, we passed weak laws to save them, added regulations and protected zones. But nobody believed they'd ever really fish them to death."

Army snorted. "Sounds familiar." Nobody had ever thought antibiotics would just stop working.

"Yep. And the climate change didn't help the cod, either. When the North Atlantic starts feeling like the Gulf of Mexico, if you don't have the strength to paddle to Greenland, you die."

Army helped him scale it, and then they both rinsed their hands and headed inside to the galley. Byron panfried half the fish and served it with a couple of the boiled eggs Rory had packed for them.

"I can remember when the reefs started to die, near the island where I grew up. First the algae tide, then the coral just . . . poof. We called them ghost towns, those reefs that used to be like an underwater jungle, all those colors. Suddenly they just became white, dead. All the fish disappeared, barely a lobster could be found." Army looked down at his empty plate and then studied Byron. "Is this cod a sign that things are getting better?"

Byron gave a smirk and shrugged. "It's bound to be better for everything but humans. We're a fraction of the number we used to be. But we managed to shift the earth's poles all by ourselves, something never known to happen so quickly in the history of the planet."

Army's stunned expression revealed he hadn't been taught this in school. Byron topped off their coffees and cleaned the plates, explaining further as Army got the boat moving again.

"We caused such extreme climate change that, by the turn of the century, the distribution of water around the earth had simply shifted. Eurasia was drained of its aquifers, and drought has plagued most of it through the last hundred years. Add to that the melting of the polar ice caps, and it's as if the earth was a spinning top and then someone stuck a piece of gum on it." He reached over to an ancient bobber hooked to a shelf, his grandfather's effort at decor. Pinching it at the top, he flicked his fingers, and it spun three times, old and uneven, then toppled. "It unbalances the distribution of weight and the top wobbles. Now, the earth has always had an imperfect spin, but we threw it into complete reversal from the direction it had always wobbled, when the pole was at the top of Canada."

"So where's the North Pole now?"

"Not far above Norway."

"And all this is why electrical storms and freak blizzards can happen without warning?" As Byron nodded and started to explain more, Army held up a hand. "I need a break."

Settling back into the pilot's seat, Army eyed his GPS coordinates with distrust. "Those still work," Byron reassured him. "Compasses have to be adjusted for."

CHAPTER 16

North of Freeport, Maine

Rory shifted her backpack, tightening the straps a little so the hefty weight sat higher on her spine. She and her parents had hiked and camped plenty before. But she'd never had to carry all her supplies to camp, sleep, eat, and survive on her back. A fact that, if she had her way, Navy was never going to find out. It had been hard enough to leave the Jeep behind, with all its memories, but it had barely limped past Portland. Instead of selling or trading it, they'd hidden it in the woods. Though she was concerned about his health, Navy had insisted they switch to travel on foot, since there was always a chance they'd missed another tracker, and any trade for another vehicle would leave behind a witness, a clue to where they were headed.

The last couple hours between them had been very quiet. Now that they were walking side by side, alone in the Maine woods, it felt even more awkward. She decided that, though she internally warned herself that she barely knew him, it was her own fault for not at least trying. Shy wasn't her style, so that left no choice but to make an effort.

"Is your pack too heavy?" he asked just as she said, "So you were a SEAL?"

Passing each other a smile, they fell into silence again, and Rory let him take the lead.

"My pack's fine."

"Good." They kept moving, and Navy waited a moment before asking, "So, what's the fish-blood oath?"

Rory huffed out a laugh. "It's an old fisherman's legend that

Birdy's family always told. The gist of it was that there was this old fisherman with a young wife, who worried she would stray and so he sought out a cure to stay young and virile. He rowed out and begged God for help. A huge old cod came to the surface—Dad always loved that part, that an endangered fish could be God or God might show up in the humble form of a fish—and made a deal with him. The fish said, 'If you drink some of my blood, you'll be virile and healthy.' So, he did."

Navy waited. "And?"

"And his payment was that he had to give his blood to the fish. He went home and his wife said he smelled mighty fishy, but she fell in love with him again. But over time, he kept coming back to make the fish-blood oath again, and he got fishier and fishier, till she left him for a new man in town. Eventually the old man turned into a fish and dove into the ocean. When he asked the other codfish where the old magic fish had gone, they say he got to smelling funny, then walked out of the ocean a man and settled down with a sweet young thing in town."

Navy chuckled at the story's quick, dark twist.

"I think the moral of the story was that if you abuse nature's gifts, it will steal your favorites back."

After a moment's internal debate and quiet hiking, Navy spoke. "I was a SEAL. Then I got recruited to work for TEAR. We were part of a recovery team that found and extracted donors. Survivors. So that they could help the researchers."

Rory studied the ground intently, processing. "*Extracted* is a word you use when someone's lost, right? Or kidnapped?"

"Yes, that's the military term. It turned out that we were the kidnappers."

"You . . . you took people from their homes?"

Navy stopped and turned to her where she stood rooted. As he closed the gap between them, his amber-green eyes held hers with that intensity that usually made warm tingles start at the bottom of her neck and move throughout her body. She wasn't feeling those now.

"Yes, Rory. I took good people from their families and put

them in harm's way—I gave them to TEAR. I can only pray they're all still okay so that I can have the chance to undo those things and make it right someday." When she didn't look away from him in revulsion, he went on, but his voice deepened to a quiet, shamed tone. "I could tell you I did it because I was misled, but that excuse isn't good enough for me. If we didn't have to discuss that time anymore, I'd rather not. But if that's not enough information to help you know you can trust me, I'll tell you more. I'll tell you whatever you want, Rory."

Rory had a difficult time finding her breath to speak as his humility made her heart hurt. "I don't—didn't mean to—cause you pain. You don't have to tell me more."

"Thank you." They resumed hiking, and after another mile Navy consulted his map and snapped open a compass. By his reckoning, they needed to angle northeast more to reach Bristol, his three-day goal point.

"You can't trust that," she said lightly of the compass as she passed him.

"What? Why not?"

"Because the pole is, like, seventeen clicks east-southeast of the needle there." After digging a small handheld GPS from the side of her backpack, she turned and pitched it to him. He caught it one-handed.

Rory shivered as a sudden, cold wind whipped through the trees, high at the forest's canopy, but detectable down on its floor, too. Maybe she had some of her father's innate skills, or perhaps all her time with him had rubbed off on her, but she had the distinct feeling that a three-day hike might become much longer. And that she had not packed for the weather that was coming in.

"What's that about the North Pole?" he shouted after her.

As dusk neared, Rory's suspicions were confirmed. The temperature had plummeted from the mid-sixties to just above thirty degrees, and the wind picked up from the north until it was lashing them like knives. Rain came with it, now freezing needles. They discussed looking for a cave or a low spot, but they were constantly rerouting around the finger-like projections that made up the rocky Maine coast. Even though the inlets were deep enough to seem more like a lake, the gusts whipping off them made the temperature even sharper. Rory's parka wasn't made for this kind of weather.

As they circled another inlet, Navy tugged her inland.

"The trees will give us a buffer from these headwinds. Let's move in."

Nodding, she ducked her head into her jacket's hood and kept it down as she followed him further west of their original direction. A howling wind that made her think of her father's love of Irish poems and banshees whined through the forest and raised the hairs on her neck for a second. In that second when she paused, a sharp blow struck her shoulder, spun her into the wind, and knocked her to her hands and knees with a cry of surprise. Her first thought was that she'd been attacked, but then she saw the piece of sheet metal bounce onto the ground and stop at a nearby tree.

Navy heard her cry of pain and a metallic clang and turned to see her kneeling, facing back east again. He saw what looked like a piece of barn metal and realized the wind must have whipped it right into her.

"Rory! Are you okay?" he asked, dropping to a knee beside her. He could see her jacket was torn through, a patch of her skin at her shoulder underneath nastily scraped with a shallow but ragged gash.

She groaned but nodded, and sank back onto her folded legs to catch her breath. Adrenaline had instantly kicked her heartbeat up. She met his steely, concerned eyes. "I have this weird feeling there's a barn nearby."

Stifling a grin, he helped her up. They reasoned the strip of metal had been carried by the wind, so they headed into it again, Navy keeping her directly behind him. He finally spotted the mossy rocks of a small building that looked to be an ancient fishing shack. Its roof was intact, but they could see where the piece of metal had peeled off the tumbledown porch.

Inside the structure was dusty but somewhat clean, watertight, and obviously left by someone who expected to return. Firewood was stacked near the tiny fireplace, fishing supplies in the corner, a card table and two chairs folded against a wall. The whole place was hardly over twelve square feet, but it was out of the wind and rain.

"Oh, my God. Do you think we could make a fire happen? I'm frozen."

Navy checked the wood. "Yeah, though it may not last for long. It's pretty dry." Rory unfolded the chairs and then started to search for matches in her bag. When he came to pull her jacket off, she jerked away with a frown.

"I'm freezing, what are you doing?"

"I need to see your shoulder."

"It's fine, I—" She couldn't finish her statement before he'd pulled her jacket off and then suddenly tugged her long-sleeved thermal over her head. The movement rubbed what she was sure was just a scratch on her right shoulder, but it stung. "Jesus, oww! Your bedside manner sucks, Navy."

"I'm more of a battlefield medic than a nurse. Sit down."

"No, I'm cold and I want to start a fire." She faced off with him, hugging her bare arms to herself, and saw the temper flare behind his deceptively flat expression.

"I said sit down, Rory."

"It's just a scratch, it'll heal fine—"

"You're not superwoman," he growled.

"You're not persuasive," she snapped.

"I have never met anyone as goddamned stubborn as you." Stalking to the fireplace, he pitched together a fire with enough force to shatter a couple of small logs, and it lit with satisfying ease as soon as his lighter touched the dry wood.

"Apparently I'm effective, too," she muttered, pulling the chair as close as she could to the fire. He ignored her and brought out the supplies they'd taken from the hospital.

Navy snapped a chair down perpendicular to hers and draped his own larger jacket around her so that only one shoulder was bare, then gently cleaned the jagged, clotted cut left by the metal. It was already bruising. He taped a bandage over it, resisting the urge to lean in and kiss the delicate collarbone.

"Thank you," she said, meeting his eyes. Then she added, "But it would have been fi—"

Navy stopped her with a finger over her lips. He interrupted her softly. "You looked after me. Maybe I like looking after you." Her blue-green eyes softened, and he felt her breath escape in surprise against his finger. His gaze strayed to her lips and she shivered. He wondered how she still felt cold, but then he realized the logs were already almost gone.

"Let me throw the rest in."

Rory was fully warmed through now, but she didn't stop him. It gave her a chance to roll her eyes to the ceiling and let out a slow, silent breath. *Stop feeling things*, she begged her heart. Being near him was becoming excruciating when he looked at her like that. *You're just the damned mission, Rory. It's his* job *to assure you're alive and unharmed.*

To take her mind off him, she searched through her bag for the food they had packed and tried to make it a little more appealing, opening and warming the cans of chili by the fire. They ate, chatting only about the severity of the storm and the number of miles they wanted to cover the next day. By the time she'd cleaned her spoon, she was feeling drowsy, so Rory rolled out her sleeping bag and made a pillow of her pack. The fire was barely embers now, but perhaps she could catch some warmth from it as she drifted off.

Navy watched her quietly as she pulled her jacket over her bag, then over her head, and finally folded herself into a ball inside her bag to stay warm. With the light of a small LED lamp, he marked the route he wanted to take tomorrow, passing a few marinas along the way. The sooner they could steal a good boat, the easier life would be for Rory. Hiking fifteen miles a day wasn't exactly her daily routine.

He rolled out his sleeping bag behind her and stretched out on his back, watching and listening to her trying to get to sleep. The storm would likely be gone tomorrow, but the temperature outside was definitely in the twenties, and it seeped through the old mortar between the rocks. Her teeth were chattering uncontrollably. He could see the shivers wracking her slim form under the useless, old sleeping bag.

"Rory."

She grunted a question back.

"Rory, come here."

"I'm fine."

"Goddammit, Rory, you're hypothermic. Come here." She unzipped her bag, and her tousled blonde head poked out to look over at him. He held open his sleeping bag in invitation, and after a hesitant moment of shivering in the open, she scooted over and slid in next to him. Navy turned on his side to accommodate them both, an arm under her neck, and zipped the bag shut.

Rory's eyes closed in bliss when Navy's two arms locked around her upper body and he slid a heavy, warm leg over hers. She still couldn't control her shaking muscles, but with each tremble he squeezed her back against his chest soothingly. Soon her teeth stopped chattering, and then the shivers slowed, and she felt as tired as if she were drugged.

"Sorry. I was so cold," she whispered. "I'll be okay in my own bag now."

"Shh. Get some rest," Navy said against her temple. "I'm not letting you go." When she let out a relieved sigh and fell promptly asleep, he smiled in the dark.

CHAPTER 17

Rory awoke disoriented, uncertain where she was. Her pillow wasn't in her favorite spot, and it wasn't soft. The day before came back to her, and she realized she had rolled into Navy. He had shifted onto his back and she to his shoulder, his arm locked tight around her. It was still dark out but showing the kind of inky blue that told her sunrise was less than an hour away.

Rory raised her face to look at him sleeping, noticing how the few days' growth of beard was starting to hide the lower part of the midnight-blue marks on his face. She wondered why he didn't grow it intentionally to hide them. His features, lean and straight, and his sharp jaw were a little softened by it, too. It fascinated her, the skin-color change, and she no longer even found it jarring. It was a clue to something. Something about the resistant infections, the antibodies, TEAR. If they had given him a cocktail of antibodies, it shouldn't have caused a lasting dermal effect. She had only ever read of that effect through treatment with colloidal silver. Maybe they'd been tinkering with vaccines?

Vaccines took her brain down another path, and for a long moment she lay staring at his jaw as her brain tried to find the connection, the pattern it knew hid in the details she hadn't learned yet.

"Rory. It's getting creepy."

She blinked, her vision blurry from staring into middle distance for too long.

"What?" she said in confusion, focusing again on him. His eyes were open and bemused.

"You've been staring at me for five minutes. Before and since I woke up."

"Sorry. I got lost."

"In my beard?"

She let out an embarrassed laugh. "It is quite lush." Realizing it was time to extract herself from the warm bag and his hold, she glanced over her shoulder. "Ahh . . . how do I . . . ?"

"Resume avoiding any contact with me?" he finished dryly for her. Despite his reluctance, he moved his arm from around her to find the sleeping bag's zipper and tug it down.

Not at all what I meant, Rory thought, *but probably perversely what I'll end up doing.*

"I'll make us some coffee," was all she said. She'd seen the old kettle on the mantel the night before, and, with the storm clearly passed, it seemed safe to go find some wood and kindling. After she'd pulled on her jacket and boots, she went out and circled the tiny building. The crisp, dry morning was beginning to reveal the damage from the prior evening's windstorm. Trees that had been covered in fall leaves yesterday were mostly bare, and broken limbs were all over the forest floor. Perfect for her needs.

Navy was impressed when she came back in with arms full of kindling and small logs, and even more so when she made campfire coffee over the fire.

"So where do you think Dad and Army are?" she inquired over the map he was studying.

He considered and said, "Best guess, they actually aren't far from us. They'll need to refuel to get to Nova Scotia, where they can refuel once more and then head toward the rig." Pointing to the open ocean to the southeast of Nova Scotia on the map, he explained, "We'll make the same trip, unless we can find a vessel with hydrofuel cells that also has terrible security, an unlikely combo. Either way, a multiday trip. The rig is like a city, it's one of the largest drilling platforms ever built, and it's in an area called the Hibernia. I think you'll like it. It's technically just a wind farm, but we do have gardens."

She smiled at him and then looked back at the map. "What are all those lines, here and here?" It looked like the sea was crossed with random tracks, as if a tractor had dragged a plow in the deep, dark cold ocean floor.

"They're the artifact lines of the deep-water sonar that maps the ocean floor. Even now, we've only mapped a fraction of the earth's underwater area. But this area is pretty well covered. It's not far from the sinking of the Titanic, though no more icebergs these days."

Rory nodded. "I saw that old movie. Real bummer." When he laughed at her, she smiled, enjoying the sound and the sight of him at ease.

"Well, it provides good cover for us. There isn't much traffic there, the wind farm keeps away most vessels in the area, and our traffic to and from the Hibernia is assumed to be tours to the Titanic graveyard." He folded up his map and returned it to his pack, adding, "Which is a great reason for us to get moving. If we could find a boat tonight, we could sail overnight and be that much closer."

In agreement, Rory finished packing her own meager belongings, and they soon set off north again. The storm had blown from the northwest toward the eastern shore and out to sea. Which meant, in her estimation, straight into the path of her father and Army. While she was sure they would be okay if they had anchored close to shore, she wished that they had a way to confirm it.

CHAPTER 18

Frenchman Bay near Bar Harbor, Maine

The anchor back on deck, Army straightened and stretched a moment. A flock of geese passed overhead, high in the sky and maintaining their imperfect V shape. In his view, the mountains of Acadia National Park were brightly lit by the morning sun, and he could see where the colors of fall had been stripped from most of the trees by the night's storm. They had hunkered down early the prior evening to wait it out, playing cards and telling tales over a few whiskeys.

Today might be their final push to reach the Hibernia, but he had heard Byron discussing a storm cell over the radio with other ships.

"They head south later every year," Byron mused from the cabin door, and Army looked up in confusion. "The geese. They used to head farther south, and far earlier in the year. Now, any farther than Virginia is the tropics to them."

Army asked, "Any of your new buddies know if we should be heading south?"

"Yep. There's a hefty dip in the polar vortex that's likely to make for rough seas tonight. If we're on our way soon, I think we'll barely feel a breeze."

Nodding, Army began to follow Byron back to the helm, but he halted when another V of geese passed above, lower in altitude.

"What?" Byron asked when he glanced back and saw Army's dark eyes burning.

"That flock was heading north."

"That's not right."

"That's not geese."

A sound came from the front of the boat, and they both slowly exited the cabin again and circled to the bow of the vessel. Perched on the deck sat seven huge geese, eerily still in a way that living animals could not be. Their eyes stared unblinking at Army and Byron.

Byron muttered, "Where's your gun?"

"It wouldn't help," Army replied. Their heads were equal to a mid-size dog's, their wingspans likely ten feet. "They're only surveillance birds."

"Well, that's surprisingly not reassuring," Byron commented. Army suddenly turned and left Byron alone with them. "Neither is that."

A few seconds later, he returned, walking slowly backward. Before Byron could ask what he was doing, Army spun toward the birds, and Byron watched the boat's old fishing net fly in a perfect cast that billowed out and landed over the birds.

"Get ready. This ain't gonna be pretty!" he shouted as he flung it.

But Byron knew immediately what his job was: to wrap the birds as tightly as he could and either crush them or drown them. When they first began to respond in a mechanical, confused movement—not the panicked flapping a normal bird might show—he grabbed the fishnet's edges closest to him as Army mirrored him across the deck. They managed to pull the net in just as the drones began to realize they should fight. The first hit he got from the bird nearly knocked Byron on his ass, and he touched his forehead to find it bleeding.

"Move it, Byron!" Army shouted. Scrambling, Byron grabbed a hooked pole on the deck that they used to catch and pull up crab traps. He shoved it through the pile of birds, hooked the back of the net behind them, and yanked it toward himself.

The movement of the net, powered by Byron's hook, knocked a few drones over, giving Army a chance to capture more edges of the net and create a real trap.

As the deadly animals tried more forcefully to slam their huge beaks into them, Byron scooted away, but with strategic intent. Once on his feet, he sprinted to the back of the boat and turned on the winch to let the anchor out. It slowly, steadily dropped out the anchor and its chain; then he stopped it and grabbed a rope on the stern meant for tying off to docks. He knotted it into the chain.

"Byron! Where the hell are you?" Army was shouting as he dodged the metal birds and tried to keep them unbalanced. With seven birds, each arguably half his strength, he was outmanned. He'd been hit twice in the thigh, and it had felt like a hammer strike.

Byron suddenly appeared beside him, wrapping a fist around the net beneath his hands, and he tied it off quickly with a warning shout of, "Let go!"

Army gave him a questioning look, then felt the pull of the rope and looked around the boat's cabin quarters to see the anchor was dropping, and the rope Byron had locked to the net was disappearing into the sea.

"Shit! Help me throw them over!" he exclaimed, quickly calculating that the weight of the birds might damage the walls of the boat, but Byron was already thinking the same. Grabbing the hooked rod again, he snagged a part of the net, and he and Army both lifted the pole to leverage the full net over the edge of the boat and into the water with a hefty splash. They watched the birds flail as they sank. Once they were about thirty feet down, beyond Army and Byron's ability to see, a series of flashes bright enough to reach the surface confirmed their electronics weren't meant for submarine use.

Army looked up to Byron. "Nice work."

Byron was still leaned over the edge of the boat, trembling with excitement and strained muscles. "We might need a new anchor."

"Oh, we're not going to be stopping again anytime soon. Cut anchor, we need to move fast."

"You think they reported our location?"

Army said, "I think in less than an hour they'll have boats deployed on our tail."

CHAPTER 19

Camden, Maine

By midday, they'd crossed through a couple of towns, found a warm meal, and asked around about boatyards. The largest by far was still miles off, but with Navy's encouragement and indulgence in an afternoon coffee, they reached it before nightfall and began looking over the pool of vessels from a nearby hill. With the cover of night, Navy expected they could determine the security obstacles to stealing a boat, and perhaps even procure one by morning. He preferred Army's unique savvy for breaking and entering boats, honed in his youth and further sharpened in the SEALs, but Navy knew enough about hot-wiring vehicles from his own misspent youth that he still had hope.

From her position on her stomach, Rory checked again that her hair was still tightly under the newsboy cap she'd had on since they set out. Though it itched, it kept her most recognizable feature hidden. Pulling the binoculars up to her eyes, she scanned over the boats: yachts large and small, boats old and new. She knew how to pilot a boat in the shallow waters off Woods Hole, but beyond the sound and the bay, she was out of her league. From her perspective, the most reasonable boat to steal was an older one that was unlikely to be missed.

"So, Navy SEAL. What's your training telling you?" she asked him. He'd been silently watching the boatyard like a hawk, and the sun was close to the horizon.

"That dark green one, third marina row from the south, eighth vessel on the dock. Looks uninhabited but kept clean. And it's subtle." Setting down his binoculars, he looked over at her. "You ready?"

She looked shocked. Sunset was creeping onto night, and she assumed it was bad timing until nightfall. The light would illuminate them fully.

"Sunset into twilight is when your eyes have the most difficulty with light. Shadows are indistinct, your pupils are trying to decide whether to contract or adapt to darkness and dilate. You can sneak right past people's vision, and they often aren't sure what they saw." Grabbing her hand, he led her down the shadiest edge of the hill and on a circuitous route toward the boats. Soon they were through the gate entrance and at the dark green boat.

"Looks open," she whispered as they crouched alongside it.

He nodded but kept observing. No signs of anyone on the boat, just an open hatch door to the bulkhead. He gave her a shrug, motioned for her to stay put, and launched himself over the keel onto the deck. The boat was less than thirty feet long, so after a quick scan and an unanswered knock on the bulkhead door, he helped her on.

"I'll check the engine, you check what supplies they have and dig for a key. Maybe we'll get lucky."

Rory nodded and headed into the darkened lower area of the boat, pulling out her flashlight and trying not to let it hit windows. She saw a small galley, coffee pot temptingly ready to start. Otherwise it seemed tidy and left ready for its next fishing expedition. The head was just past it, and then the door to a sleeping quarters stood ajar. *Where would I hide keys?* she wondered. As she walked to the sleeping quarters, her light caught the rows of drawers under the bed, and she knelt and dug through them, but found only socks and swim trunks.

Standing, she ran her light over the bed, and the scene there confused her momentarily as her brain tried to process it. A dog, old and sweetly gray-faced, lay turned toward her. She jumped when she realized the owner lay behind him, arm draped over his furry neck and head tucked against the dog's. Then she saw the gun. And then she saw the blood.

Navy jumped when she ran past him to the stern of the boat

and leaned over the rail, making a sound like she was fighting a sob or trying to breathe after a punch.

"What's wrong?"

"It can't be this one. It can't be this boat." She said it desperately, then covered her mouth and pointed to the bulkhead. She closed her eyes and turned her head away from him. Navy headed down into it with her flashlight.

As best Navy could tell, they had only been dead a couple of days or less. The bullet had been aimed for certain death, designed to kill the dog and then its owner in the same second, a shot under the old pup's jaw through into his master's forehead. Maybe he had been infected and suspected he wouldn't survive. But he hadn't left his canine companion to an uncertain future.

Rory had already controlled her tears when he folded her into his arms and held her for a long moment.

"I'm sorry, Rory. I'm sorry you found that instead of me."

"It's okay." With a deep breath, she whispered, "It's awful and yet somehow . . . beautiful at the same time." He tucked a loose strand of hair back behind her ear and under the cap.

"You've got your dad's sensitive heart. Okay, now it's your turn to pick a boat." Navy knew the best way to recover from a death scene was humor.

"What? I'm only an amateur boat thief. I have no opinion."

"Sure you do. If not, you need to."

She sent him an arch look.

"I mean it," he pressed. "Byron should have taught you more. You should know how to use a gun, and how to steal a boat won't be a bad skill either." Rory searched his amber eyes but saw only the hard-assed Navy who seemed to live to challenge her.

Turning her gaze around the dark boatyard, she scanned it hopefully. "All right. What about the one under tarps over there? It's low to the water, like it might be a catamaran. Those are stable, right? It isn't huge, but if it has a decent engine it would get us there safely."

He looked surprised. "Good reasoning. I wondered the same.

The tarp tells me it's also probably very, very valuable. Meaning it would be quickly missed by the boatyard manager." Looking at the covered boat, he added, "But if it's valuable, it's fast."

In a few moments they had moved quietly over to the other boat, and Navy began removing the huge tarp. She observed the way he detached it at each cleat and began to copy him on the sides she could reach, but she froze when she heard a distant tick and a buzzing noise. On the far end of the docks, the darkest spot of the large marina, lights were clicking on. They were slowly lighting up in succession, a wave of artificial light moving toward them. And following that wave, a night watchman had appeared from the manager's shed, performing his nightly round. He was listening to music on earbuds, but they would soon be unable to miss when the lights reached them.

"Damn," she cursed. "It must be on a sensor." She glanced at Navy, who only tried to work faster. Thinking quickly, she dug deep into her pack and pulled out a small handgun. Kneeling behind a low pier post along the dock, she steadied her arms on the post and fired the quiet weapon with a soft pop. The light nearest them cracked, rendering the still-dark light useless. She worked toward the night watchman, shooting out each light with the small pistol. Navy paused to observe, amazed, as the watchman stopped and examined each light turning off with a tempo that hinted at an electrical problem. He grumbled curses and then headed back to the manager's office.

Rory shifted on her heels and straightened into Navy's chest.

"What was that?" He was grinning.

She could feel herself blush in the dark. "It's a BB gun. I use it to get quail sometimes. I didn't want you to make fun of me."

Navy grabbed her face with both hands and kissed her once, hot and hard.

"C'mon. I'm going to tow her out to the edge of the marina and shove off. Then you're going to learn how to hot-wire a boat. You won't believe this boat."

Rory followed him to where he'd peeled back half of the boat cover to reveal black, glassy panels with recognizable grid patterns covering every horizontal surface. The name on the rear center of the catamaran was in a modern script: *Solar Stealth.*

She looked up at him in amazement. "It's a solar-powered cat?"

Nodding, he threw an arm around her shoulder and hugged her close. "Nice choice, babe."

Navy managed to hot-wire the engine and get the auxiliary hydrofuel cell motor running. They headed north along the coastline, staying a couple miles off the coast, while Rory explored the boat. Meant for only two to four travelers, it had a tiny bed tucked into the bow and a convertible table-to-bed in the galley. It was stocked with some canned and dry foods and had a small but useful galley that yielded a pot of coffee to warm them while they tried to determine where the heaters turned on.

"Hot coffee. I saw supplies for fishing and crabbing, plus a saltwater-to-drinking-water converter in some cabinets."

"That's good. If the sun comes up and skies are clear, maybe we can avoid stopping." Navy sipped the coffee she'd made and settled into the pilot's chair of the cat while she found a bench seat folded against the wall opposite the helm. As she held her coffee over bent knees, her hands shook so hard that the coffee sloshed out. He took her mug and set it aside, squeezing both her hands in one of his. "It's the adrenaline wearing off. You reacted really well in a crisis, Rory." He squeezed her hands again, then let go, and Rory felt her stomach do the seesaw it did whenever he veered back into keeping a cool distance from her.

She let out a chuff of a laugh. "Many generations will tell the tale of the BB gun that saved a SEAL."

He sent her a warm smile that had tingles replacing the shakes in her hands. *Seesaw,* she thought.

"You're a damn fine shot. I'll show you how to use my gun if we ever get a chance to stop swimming and just tread water."

Rory watched him scanning the moonlit horizon, the fancy boat's complex displays, at complete ease while at complete attention. She tipped her head. "What's your real name?"

"Nathaniel Adrien Vercoeur."

She put it together far faster than he expected. "N.A.V."

He shot her an impressed glance. "We had another Nate in my platoon, last name Victor. His last name made for problematic communications, so he got the nickname *Nav* and I got Navy." He adjusted speed as the waves got rougher and sent her a glance. "You thought I would lie to you."

"I thought you would avoid me," she said after a hesitation.

"I have never avoided you, Rory."

Faced with that cryptic and warmly delivered insight, Rory decided she was too tired to try to figure him out. "I'm going to try to scrape together a meal in the galley." As she headed back, he grabbed her hand.

"Wait. Rory, I . . ." but Navy couldn't finish it as he wanted. *I'm crazy about you and I can't seem to tell you. I am hiding things from you, but it's for your own good. I hate keeping anything from you, and I crave every question you ask.*

Instead he said, "I need your help here. This weather radar, can you read it? I know what it's hinting at, but I can't tell how bad that storm is."

Rory leaned in, and the smell of her hair made his hand clench tightly against the need to touch her. Much more time in these close quarters, and the heat between them was going to make up for the lack of a heater onboard.

Scanning the areas of low pressure and cold air flowing down from the Pole, Rory recalled mnemonics and lessons Byron had tried to impart.

"That's not good. Especially considering last night. This is probably a dip in the polar vortex. It's not unusual for this time of year or this area, but the pressure differential could mean rough seas and really high winds. If I were you, I'd want to tuck into a cove and drop anchor for the night, but can we?" She raised blue-green eyes to his and suddenly lost her breath at how close they were, at the hunger in his eyes.

His mind got lost in her nearness, so he reverted to training, turned off that part of his brain, and focused on the screen. He weighed the risk, how far they'd traveled from the marina, the nearest coves on the map, and their relative safety. Then he estimated the amount of battery they had before the sun reached their solar cells. He considered stopping now, the worst-case scenarios. In them, Rory ended up in the hands of TEAR. It was an unacceptable possibility.

"We need to get as far as possible before the sun is up. Do you think that storm is headed out to sea or sweeping back north?"

Rory flinched at his sudden switch to cold, calculating soldier. Looking back to the computer, she studied it again and tried to find more info on other screens, but ultimately she was forced to guess. "Out. But even if it heads north, if we head for that bay, we should be sheltered."

"Bay of Fundy," Navy pointed to the body of water between New Brunswick and Nova Scotia. "That's where I first learned to pilot a boat."

Washington, DC, TEAR Headquarters

Kessler sat behind his desk, tapping a vintage Montblanc against his desktop in a steady, slow rhythm that tested the nerves of his officers in the room. They were waiting—had been waiting—for an update from the analysts since before sunset. Finally a wrist phone pinged, and they all check theirs. Both the officers turned their wrists up, and the screen illuminated on their forearms. They glanced at one another in hesitation.

"Oh, just tell me what the fuck is going on," Kessler barked. "Have they found them?"

"No. The farm appears abandoned. The boat is gone, and they're trying to track it down. A flock of drones scouring the coast was lost after reporting a set of images that match the husband of Dr. Tyler-Stevigson and the SEAL."

"Which SEAL?"

"Army Harrison."

"She's with the other. They would split camps, head different directions and use different travel methods." Kessler waved a hand. "Basic black ops training."

"They are expanding the search quadrants, monitoring their known wireless devices, but right now, the climatologist and Army Harrison appear to be traveling alone, north along the Atlantic coast."

"And the girl is lost?"

Silence confirmed his suspicion. The pen began to tap slowly again.

"He's going to ground. He's turned off coms. Traveling by foot, probably. But where is he taking her, and why? She must know whatever her mother knew that made her leave TEAR and go all native. Then *he* would have told her more." Kessler scoured his brain for what they knew about Persephone Tyler-Stevigson, but the only face that came to his mind was Rajni's. Dr. Rajni, who had defended her and wanted his staff to share less about her. "Find Dr. Rajni. Interrogate him, and get every bit of info he knows about that girl. Tonight."

CHAPTER 20

Northern Atlantic, East of Matinicus Island

She was lucky enough to find cans of tuna, crackers, and old packets of mayo—enough to create a passable meal, while the waves grew in intensity and the wind buffetted the craft with a giant's strength. The storm closed in on them through the satellite-linked dashboard and manifested itself inside the small vessel by making it difficult to make much headway. As she took their dishes to the sink, a sudden wave threw the boat high and sideways on one of its twin hulls. It tossed Rory sideways, and she rapped her head against a cabinet before she could brace herself. The cabinet popped open, revealing the power console she'd been seeking earlier.

Hearing the noise, Navy shouted her name and tried to lean away from the helm enough to see her without letting go of the wheel.

"I'm fine, I'm fine. I found the heater switches," she said dryly. She was still rubbing her head when she came back to her seat. "I think I'll just sit still."

"Good. And leave the heater off until we stop. It'll feel even colder when we're not moving."

Rory tucked into her fold-down seat, wrapping her jacket tightly against the growing chill. Outside, the wind and the waves became living things, rearing up ahead of them at heights too tall even to be illuminated by the boat's lights. Navy seemed to feel his way through them, trusting an instinct that told him where to steer for the lowest point, while keeping them faced into the waves' path. To Rory, it felt as if sea monsters were continuously appearing through the wide windows, growing slowly and menacing as if ready to eat them alive. Her fear would crawl up her spine and press her chest; then Navy's instinct would take them over the monster and down its watery black back, and her fear would ebb as the inky ocean grew a new head.

He steered them through five straight hours of the roughest seas she'd ever experienced, both of them nearly silent as he focused on nothing but the ocean and the instruments. When the building-sized waves finally began to smooth into huge swells and then choppy whitecaps that were manageable on autopilot, he stepped back, stretched, and rubbed his neck to release knots of tension.

"We're pulling into Great Seal Cove to drop anchor, and it should be safe to get the heater running."

"Thank God." She shivered and crossed to the galley where she'd found the switches to flip on the boat's heater. Returning, she leaned against the passageway to the helm and watched him guide the boat into the harbor, find a spot out of the wind, and let the anchor out to keep them there safe. It struck her that, yet again, Navy had delivered her through a gauntlet that would have killed her without him.

"You keep saving my life. Thank you," she said from the doorway. "I know I'm just the mission, but I appreciate it."

Navy went silent and still, staring at the consoles. When he spoke, his voice seemed to resonate through the quiet, tiny cabin, and made the space between them feel even smaller.

"Is that the problem here, Rory? You think I regard you as a mission?"

She dodged the question. "I didn't say there was a problem."

He looked over at her, pinning her with amber eyes that read her mind.

"Then why do you watch me like a hawk, avoid touching me, and question my motives constantly inside that head of yours?" Before she could answer, he stepped closer to her. "Maybe you've convinced yourself that I only care enough to deliver you from Point A to Point B?"

His eyes didn't look like those of a man who was only finishing a job. With the dark marks on his face shadowed by a few days' growth of beard, his shirt still stained from the blood of a wound he'd acquired defending her life, and his eyes burning into hers . . . he seemed suddenly determined. As her heartbeat quickened, her cheeks flamed, and she wondered if the SEALs taught him how to hear those things better than mere humans could. A tiny lift at the side of his mouth confirmed that suspicion.

She swallowed. "Aren't you?" she managed. His eyebrow rose. "Aren't I what?"

Shit, she thought. *I can't even remember what he was saying. Get it together, Rory!*

"Just going to drop me at the research station and disappear. Why else do you suddenly switch from being soldier to eyeing me like . . . and back again?"

He moved closer, cocking his head. "Like what, Rory? Like I want to eat you alive?" She lost her breath and took a step back in pace with him. "Like I want to peel off your clothes and touch every inch of you? Like I can't get you out of my head, and I'm just waiting for you to realize how I feel about you?"

Each step brought him closer, his broad shoulders blocking out everything else. She took a careful step backward. "What are you doing?" she whispered. It was hard enough to keep pace with his steps, but his conversation had left her head and heart spinning. She felt like a tightrope walker about to tumble to an uncertain fate, with no net and a perverse desire to jump anyway.

"I'm moving toward you slowly."

"Why?"

"I think if I ran, we'd both get hurt."

Now he was inches from her, and she'd backed herself into the corner of the galley. The tightrope wobbled; she jumped anyway. Pushing off the countertop, she closed the gap between them and met his mouth with hers as she wrapped her hands around his neck. His arms closed crushingly around her, his lips devouring hers with the hunger she'd been sensing, doubting, from him.

Sensations assaulted her as he pressed her against the wall, his lips leaving hers only to travel down her throat while his hands roamed down her sides, over her hips, and under her thighs to hoist her legs around his waist.

"You drive me insane. I could never just leave you," he growled into the curve of her throat. "How could you think that?" Rory tried to answer, but he covered her lips with his, and his hands slid into her hair as his mouth explored hers. She hardly registered that he was also cradling her head as he carried them to the sleeping berth of the catamaran.

CHAPTER 21

Bethesda, Maryland, TEAR Lab Headquarters

Dr. Jason Rajni let out a hiss of pain as the officer slammed him back into the seat he had just stood up from.

"You can't keep me here. I've done nothing to deserve this."

"You'll stay until all our questions are answered."

"I've. Answered. Them." Rajni bit out the words in fury. "I only know Persephone gave her daughter shots."

"What did she give the girl?" the officer repeated.

"I told you, I was never sure what they were!"

"Tell me more about when you and Persephone last spoke, before her death."

Rajni sighed. This was the fourth retelling.

"Persephone asked about the clinical trials. She'd been digging into my databases and suspected it, but she had no proof." His mind recalled far more than he shared. Persephone finding the human test subjects, accusing him of abandoning all ethics.

You didn't lose a child! he had screamed at her. *Ethics be damned.*

"She said I had abandoned my ethics," he recounted, "and I told her that she didn't lose a child, and her ethics could be damned. I didn't see her or communicate with her again before she died." Rajni was a well-read man. He knew the best liars wove truth throughout their fictions. And he had abandoned his ethics. He had left them at the hospital bedside of a four-year-old boy with his curly dark hair and his wife's soft brown eyes. If TEAR could keep the rest of his family from dying, or another parent from feeling his soul-destroying grief, he would cross almost any moral boundary they asked.

The door opened and a familiar face met his. Kessler.

Kessler pulled up a chair and offered him one of the two coffees he was holding.

"Dr. Rajni," he said with a nod.

"General Kessler. I thought perhaps you trusted me enough not to treat me like a petty criminal."

"I can count on one hand those I trust in this world, Doctor," Kessler chuckled. "And the only one that isn't dead is my dog."

"I've been here repeating myself to your officers for over an hour. My wife will wonder where I am."

"I've heard. And for what it's worth, I believe you. So I have one last question."

"Please. Do go on."

Kessler wasn't accustomed to anyone's disrespect. Though tempted, he restrained himself from throttling Rajni and took a soothing breath.

"If you don't know what shots the girl was given, surely you know whether there's any scientific possibility for her to be resistant to infections."

Rajni paused and tipped his head. "That's what you think is going on? That Aurora Stevigson is some sort of . . . walking cure?"

Kessler shook his head in mock shock before his features settled into a flat, emotionless expression that caused a frisson of terror to climb through Rajni. "Don't act stupid. Yes, of course that's what I'm fucking asking. Is it possible?" Rajni was quite certain the man could, and would, kill him without hesitation or remorse.

"Anything is possible. It's highly, highly, highly improbable." Rajni leaned back, feigning the relaxation he didn't feel. "For example, if in fact Persephone's daughter had some sort of magic blood, the very simple logic would follow that Persephone would not have died of an infection."

"Why not?"

"Don't act stupid, General. It's not logical for the same reason that you and I are keeping patients in forced comas while we use them for their blood antibodies like some sort of twisted human dairy farm."

CHAPTER 22

Great Seal Cove, North Atlantic

Sunlight pierced the small side windows of the sleeping bunk and woke Rory slowly. It had been a long time since she'd slept on a boat. She'd forgotten the lullaby of waves splashing against a hull. She had never woken, undressed, in a man's arms.

Sliding her head back, she examined Navy's sleeping face. He looked completely relaxed, peaceful. It was the first time she'd ever seen him like that. She wanted to let him sleep, but she couldn't resist touching him again.

Navy lay still, letting Rory's fingertips whisper over his chest and abdomen as she traced the dark discolorations of his skin. Was she regretting her decision in the light of day? Then her lips replaced her fingertips, kissing a trail along one of the blue marks.

It was more than he could take. With a laughing groan, he dragged her closer and rolled her across his chest to pin her beneath him. She let out a squeal of surprise and laughter when he buried his face in her neck. When his lips began to trail across her collarbones and down her chest, the laughter turned into sighs carrying his name.

His body fit into hers perfectly, extending the waking dream and pushing away reality a little longer until she let out a cry of pleasure and her nails dug into his shoulders to anchor her to the earth.

"Good morning, Rory," he whispered a few moments later, and she giggled again.

"Good morning, Navy."

Rory rolled with him onto their sides and touched his face as their eyes held.

"When do we have to leave?" she asked.

"Not soon. The batteries died around three, and we need the charge time."

She blinked blue-green eyes. "How did you . . . ?"

"I heard the heater go off." He grinned. "I guess you were too warm to notice."

She kissed him to linger in the warmth.

"C'mon. I'll show you Great Seal Cove," he suggested. "We can buy some supplies, if the store is still here."

"Did you come here when you were young?"

Navy nodded and recalled the long fishing trips with his father. Cold, wet, hard work. But looking back, it was the purest, most honest work he'd ever done.

"I drank my first whiskey at the tavern here." She wondered if he even realized he was twisting a lock of her hair in his fingers. "Yeah, my father and I came here on fishing trips," he finally explained.

"Are you hungry?"

His smile was wolflike. "Starving, since I met you."

Rory laughed and pushed up to sit on the edge of the bed. "If there's no store, no restaurant or diner or even a farm with eggs, I might be eating Atlantic sushi for breakfast."

After finding a dockside store, they tied off the cat and loaded up on fresh food, then walked through the small town built around the cove's inner harbor. The town's only restaurant was open, and they both devoured large plates of eggs, smoked fish, and potatoes. A small fishing shop yielded some bait and a new, warmer jacket for Rory.

He took her hand as they walked, and Rory indulged in fantasy for a moment: that she was a normal young woman, on a vacation with her lover, enjoying a beautiful stroll. The urge to beg him to stay there with her was almost as strong as the longing she had to tell her mother what she was experiencing.

"I wish you could have met my mother. She would have liked you."

Navy paused, and she turned, surprised to find him staring at her intently. He tugged her into his arms and held her tightly. Into her hair he whispered, "Sorry. I was just thinking the same thing about my dad."

After a moment's silence, she tilted her head back to meet his kiss.

"Did your dad teach you how to catch lobster? Because as far as I've seen, you're awful at it."

Laughing, he pressed her forward to return to the boat.

"He really would have liked you."

Back on the boat, as they cast off and Navy checked the displays again to set their course, he turned the radio on low to listen to the chatter of the other boats. When Rory sent him a questioning look, he explained.

"We're going to curve past the southern tip of Nova Scotia, and it's a busy area. I want to know how much Coast Guard activity there is, because that's the next logical step for TEAR. Kessler will tell them to look for stolen boats and go from there."

Rory listened along with him, hoping to hear her father's baritone cut through the lines and confirm he was all right. The thought of joining a new world, a new place with its own new cultural norms, people, and relationships, seemed more than daunting without him. She was sure he was safe, but she'd prefer he be with her when they switched from the boat to their new destination.

"What's eating at you?" Navy interrupted her thoughts with a gentle nudge.

She met his eyes and shrugged. "I just don't know anything about this place we're going. I'd like to disembark knowing Dad is there already, or arrive with him."

He nodded. "Ask me anything about it."

"I don't know . . . tell me what it's like. Who founded the Resistance? What type of people have joined it?"

Navy turned the radio down slightly and gave a few seconds' thought before launching in with the facts he was willing to share.

"I'd say it came together with a handful of scientists who became aware of what TEAR was doing and its real agenda. Jeffrey McWray, an ex-Marine and technology and energy billionaire, got involved early, gave access to resources we wouldn't otherwise have—that's what the Hibernia really is, his energy farm."

"Like a wind farm?"

"There are those. Also wave farming, capturing kinetic energy of waves. Byron's going to enjoy Jeff. That, or they'll annoy the hell out of each other. But you asked about people. Obviously me and Army. Several hackers and computer analysts. They've been watching your database. They're impressed," he added with a smile at her. "And then, of course, there are researchers. A few from TEAR, but from several other countries, too. I don't understand everything they're doing—looking at viral resistance markers or something all the time. I read the reports, but it doesn't all translate."

"Bacterial resistance markers," she supplied. His arched brow said it was still lost in translation. "Viruses don't become resistant. I mean, they could if we had drugs for them, but generally we—anyway, they aren't actually alive, so markers—I'm still confusing you, aren't I?" She laughed and rolled her eyes.

"Try again. I like when you explain the science to me." Now her brow arched. "You have sexy brains."

A smirk belied her pleasure at the comment. "Bacteria develop resistance to antibiotics after they are exposed long enough, because bacteria are constantly evolving and replicating. If you think about how long it took humans and animals to evolve to the current state—millions upon millions of generations and selection pressures that favored us walking upright, growing big, sexy brains— well, that's like a year or even a day in the life of bacteria. They replicate so quickly, and they're so simple compared to us, that overexposure to antibiotics is a selection pressure that favors the bacteria that have developed resistance. It kills off the bacteria that aren't resistant, leaving plenty of space for the smarter ones."

Navy shook his head and interrupted, "I always get this up to this point. What confuses me is how they get smart. Aren't they just single cells?"

Rory grinned. "Yes, it's true, they are. And saying they're smart is really just microbiologists giving them personalities they don't actually have. They aren't smart, they just replicate so fast that mutations that took millennia to happen for humans take only a couple weeks for them. We can't keep up with them. And viruses, well— they're even faster. They hijack our cells and use them to make copies of themselves. In all that copying, they change constantly. Which is why viruses have caused fewer deaths than other pathogens, generally."

"Lost me again. Right there at the end. I thought viruses were pretty gnarly."

"They can start that way. And certainly a few have stayed that way, because we managed to isolate their spread. But a virus that kills its host is generally at a disadvantage, evolutionarily speaking. A sick but living person spreads more germs than a dead one. It's far better to live with your host, let it sort of incorporate you, and coexist, than to wage war on it. In fact, there's evidence that our own DNA is chock-full of old viruses. Little hitchhikers that found a forever home."

Navy laughed at her metaphor. "You're going to be right at home with the team."

Something tickled at the back of Rory's brain, that feeling again that something was about to make sense to her before she'd even dived into the research she now was more than eager to be a part of at the Hibernia.

"Did you say something about viral markers?"

"Yeah, I know I read that somewhere."

"Are they working on viral vectors for gene therapy? Or maybe phage therapy? How big is the lab?"

She was surprised when he leaned over, wrapped a hand behind her neck, and kissed her hard and fast.

"Really sexy brains." Returning to the wheel, he added, "And I have no clue. Maybe when—"

Abruptly Rory dove in front of him, turning up the radio to amplify the chatter happening in the Nova Scotia harbor. Her expression seemed excited, not concerned. She grabbed the handset and pressed the button, her lips just forming the words, and he quickly snatched it.

"No names, Rory," he said sharply.

"I *know*," she snapped, grabbing it back, then took a breath.

She spoke into it with a lilting, almost giddy voice.

"'Wild nights, wild nights! Were I with thee, wild nights should be our luxury. Futile the winds to a heart in port. Done with the compass! Done with the chart!'"

She released the button and listened to the crispy silence of the open radio air as her missive left all but one of its listeners stumped.

A brief crackle responded, then Byron's voice boomed back over the airwaves. "'Rowing in Eden—Ah, the sea! Might I but moor tonight, in thee?'"

The dazzling grin that spread across her face hit Navy like a punch in the chest. She'd found Byron and Army, lacking anything more than a shortwave marine radio and poetry.

"And how is Emily's post?" Byron said after a minute.

"Quite right," she returned. "*E tu?*"

"Good. Beware north-flying geese. They're vicious."

Pleased to know he was fine, she handed off the handset to Navy, who pressed the button and said briefly, "DNR until approach. Repeat, DNR until approach."

"HUA," Army's voice replied, verbal military shorthand for a nod. Navy set the handset back in its cradle.

Since he knew she would ask, he explained. "Do not rendezvous. We have about a day and a half of travel left. I don't want to give any more drones an obvious target. It sounds like they've already seen some."

Rory found herself looking out, scanning for the shapes of birds.

He saw the direction of her searching gaze scanning the skies. "They could be underwater, too."

– 120 –

PART THREE

Rough Waters

CHAPTER 23

Washington, DC, TEAR Headquarters

"If you need me to tell you your next step, I'll be finding you a new post faster than you can call your wife and ask how she likes camel races in 140-degree Qatar."

General Kessler turned from the window he was staring out.

Kessler's top reporting officer twitched in his seat and hesitated for a moment, but he committed to an effort.

"Sir, I believe the ideal next step, in consideration of the primary target's status as unlocated, would be to return to their original location for a full sweep." He imagined his wife's face reacting to the news of a transfer out of the elite DC social circles she'd just begun to penetrate.

"Good call, soldier. Get a team down there today. Interview neighbors, too. The time for discretion is over. Dismissed."

As the door clicked behind the officer, Kessler was reading an message from the chair of the Senate Health Committee, the only committee to surpass the Senate Intelligence Committee in sheer power.

Rumors are swirling that you've let a cure slip out of the net. WTF is happening? Make something happen, or it's your head on the block.

CHAPTER 24

Hibernia Wind and Energy Farm

Rory stood next to Navy in the elevator, Army and Byron in front of them, as the lift took them to the above-water levels of the re-structured drilling platform. After days at sea, she still felt the ground moving beneath her, but her disorientation related more to the anxiety of starting a new life in such a remote, lonely place. The horizons around the platform were all the same: blue ocean and wind towers.

Navy's hand covered and threaded his fingers into hers. She felt her breath catch, then calm, as a wave of love went though her. She looked over to him and saw the corners of his mouth turn up as he squeezed her hand reassuringly.

The elevators slid open, and she saw a couple of figures in the room ahead of them. A tall, broad-shouldered man with silver-white hair stood with hands in pockets of cargo pants. As her father stepped forward, she saw a woman with dark blonde hair that waved back from a face shaped like hers.

"Mom . . ." The word left her chest like a ghost escaping.

"Rory. By. Thank God." Persephone stepped forward hesitat-ingly, but Byron crushed her in a hug before she could say another word. Their long-held love was evident as the tall man's voice cracked with tears and his hands roamed over her face, murmuring how much he'd missed her. How he thought he'd never see her again.

Rory moved into the fold, and Byron locked her into their hug, all of them now crying, though Rory still hadn't found her voice.

Her mother clasped Rory's face in her hands, her mirrored blue-green eyes devouring the sight of her daughter.

"I've missed you so, so, so much. I'll explain everything, I'm so sorry, but it was to keep you safe. God, you're so beautiful to see again."

"Mom." It was all she could manage. She didn't even feel the tears cascading off her cheeks. They locked themselves to one another as Rory felt her breath shorten with the overwhelming feelings. Opening her eyes again, she saw her father wiping his eyes helplessly.

"I've been waiting so long to see my girls together again."

Rory blinked away tears and slowly released her mother, holding her father's gaze.

"You've been waiting?" she repeated. She was in such shock, it only slowly began to come together in her mind. "You knew?" she asked Byron, and his expression was so pitying that she had to look away, to her mother. She wore the same expression of guilt and pity. Rory stepped back from them, hand to heart. "You both . . . you both faked her death . . . ? You told me she was sick. Told me she got sick so fast, while I was hiking with Birdy."

She couldn't stand to see how they were pitying her, these people she loved so desperately, who had fooled her and broken her life in half three years ago. The roar of thoughts and emotions in her brain was deafening. Persephone came toward her, appealing in the timeless approach of a mother who has caused her child to cry but knows she is the perfect one to soothe. Rory held up a palm and stepped back, into Navy's hold on both of her arms.

She looked down at his hands, the strong and warm fingers that had guided her safely here. Persuaded her, without disclosing the one reason that would have held the most sway. Lied.

"Rory. Take a slow, deep breath. You're hyperventilating," he whispered as he turned her to face him and his hands cradled her jaw.

"You, too. You knew, too." Her lungs spasmed against the combined pain of so many betrayals, of her own stupidity. She remembered how she'd slept for nights on the ground over her mother's grave, how long it had taken to be able to think of her without crying. How she had punished herself for not being there to say goodbye.

"Rory, breathe. Breathe slowly. Calm down," he said in a firmer tone, but when she met his eyes, the marked face she'd let herself fall in love with seemed one more enormous con. A deception to coax her here.

Before she could indulge more self-hatred and grief, her vision grayed at the edges, and his face faded to black.

Navy sat with his elbows resting on his knees, his chin on his folded hands, as he listened to Persephone and Byron debate their parental choices. Jeff sat in a chair as well, but he was relaxed and listening in what Navy knew was smug bemusement. He'd never had children and seemed to hold a self-assured opinion that his was a superior choice.

"That's what we discussed when we decided it. There was no way I was going to let her see my body." Persephone paced, angry, defensive, and ashamed at turns.

"I should never have agreed to it. She'll never trust us again." Byron had repeated this lament for the past few minutes as they waited for Rory to come to.

Jeff finally spoke, filling the silence. "She's less than thirty years old. There's probably not a single statement you could make about Rory that might not pivot by 180 degrees in the next five years. She'll get over this, and she'll do it quickly because everyone's depending on her."

"That's an unfair burden to put on her after all this," Persephone argued. "It's not like she understands this research better than we do."

"Perhaps she does." Jeff let the suggestion sink in. Persephone and Byron might be brilliant, but he doubted their combined genetic offspring would disappoint. Then Jeff, in his usual trouble-stirring way, gave a shrug and said, "What do you think, Navy?"

He didn't even lift his gaze to Jeff. The sight of Rory turning boneless and collapsing against him had left him shaken, and he wasn't sure his decisions along the path to that moment were very defensible.

"Why are you asking him?" Persephone asked sharply.

"I think Navy has a . . . a good grasp on Aurora's point of view. He lost his father suddenly."

"Don't play games, Jeff," Navy snapped. "There's been enough already."

"What's that supposed to mean?" Persephone snapped back.

"It means she deserves everyone's honesty. She'll deal from there." Navy pushed up from his seat and went back into the small room devoted to medical care, where they'd laid Rory down. She'd been completely unconscious, so he was surprised to see her standing at the tiny sink, splashing water on her face. She straightened to face him. Her eyes were red, and her irises glowed greener than he'd ever seen them.

Navy knew that once the others followed him in, the chance to explain anything would vanish. But speaking would let them know she was awake, and he sensed she didn't want that any more than he. He stepped closer, pleading with his eyes for her to understand that he hadn't meant to hurt, to deceive her. Navy reached for her hand. *Trust me, please.*

She snatched it back and gave a short shake of her head. Her eyes betrayed her tightly set jaw, filling with tears against her will, chin lifting in defiance of her own emotions as she drew a shaky breath.

"Mom, Dad. I'm fine," she said aloud. Navy stepped back when they rushed inside. As they began to pour out apologies, she raised a slim hand. "Stop it. What you did was . . . horrible. I can't fathom understanding why you did it, but even if I could, it would still be hard to forgive."

"Sweetheart, we won't expect forgiveness—" Byron began, but she raised a hand again.

"You'll all understand if I want some space. Mom . . . and you must be Jeff? How about the short tour to my room? I need privacy." Her tone was flat, exhausted, the voice of someone who had just lost more than she could process. As she walked out behind Jeff, she stopped and turned her head slightly back to them. "Navy was right about one thing. Everyone had better be goddamned honest from here on."

CHAPTER 25

Rory rubbed her eyes and refocused on the text she was reading on the screen, comparing it with the data she had been compiling. Things were getting bleary, her eyes dry. She absentmindedly grabbed the water nearby and glugged a few swallows, then tried to read again.

"Eventually you'll need reading glasses."

She turned to see her mother leaning against the doorway into the lab that had become Rory's new workday space. Persy shrugged and added, "I'm quite certain you have my eyes. But exhaustion is probably more the reason right now. You need a break, sweetie."

Rory found reason to smile whenever her mom was around. Three years without getting to see her would leave a scar forever, but it certainly gave her a new appreciation of her mother's presence. Her father was still not the recipient of her smiles, and she spent many sleepless nights trying to reconcile the idea that for three years he had hid Persy from her.

After a couple of weeks at the Hibernia, she was already entrenched in the research team's efforts to discover what about her immune system was different from other survivors of infections. The team, a hodgepodge mix of outstanding minds, had been unsure of her at first, but they quickly recognized her speedy grasp of the data and natural curiosity would be a needed fresh perspective. She sensed she was getting closer to solving it, that feeling of some revelation within her grasp. But her current knowledge of microbiology, immunology, and the insight from her database still didn't explain it.

"Have you eaten dinner?"

Rory shook her head. "I'll make a sandwich later."

"You can't keep avoiding him."

"I'll talk to Dad when I feel ready," Rory repeated a refrain she'd used for a fortnight. "I get that you two felt I could be taken if they thought you were alive. I just . . . He lied even when I was heartbroken over losing you."

Persy came in and sat across from her daughter, holding her eyes with those of a matching sea green. "Heartbroken was better than stolen, in a coma, your life being sucked away slowly." She took a slow breath. "But I wasn't talking about Dad. I was talking about Nathan."

Rory turned her chair away, but Persy stopped her and turned it back.

"Both of you look miserable. I mean, Nathan always looks a little stoic, but I'd be blind not to see him watching you every time your paths cross. Byron told me he sensed it at the farm, too." Persy touched her daughter's proud cheekbones with a caressing hand. "And you are not sleeping, not eating enough. Why don't you talk to him?"

"He lied to me, too." It was a cold, hard statement, and accusatory in its delivery.

Persy's eyebrows rose. "I ordered him to lie to you. My choice wasn't his story to tell you." She seemed to realize she was turning harsh instead of comforting, and it was certainly a fallback to her parental role as disciplinarian where Byron was the softer influence. "Sweetie, there's so much more I need to tell you about what brought me here. It was you, it was all you, but it was such a scary time because I feared they would kill me and take you. I left, and you know what I brought with me?"

Rory shook her head.

Persy caressed her daughter's face again. "A photo of you and Dad, and my TEAR badge. Because I knew that I needed to re-mind myself that *I was complicit* in what they were doing. I still think they've killed more people than I or Nathan ever knew. Imagine how he must feel, knowing his actions directly stole people from their families? So when I ordered him to retrieve you and Byron, it was because no one is more capable of keeping you safe, and no one more badly deserved atonement for tearing families apart by bringing ours back together."

Then she added, "I certainly didn't order him to fall in love with you, but I can forgive him for it. What happened between you two?"

"Mom, that's private." She sighed and glanced at her laptop screen again. "I can't trust him, that's the end of it. There's nothing more to tell."

Persy shrugged. "All right. I'll drop it. But I won't drop you eating dinner. Go freshen up, change out of that shirt because it smells like you slept in it for three nights, and come down to the mess hall. Someone caught a bunch of snow crabs and they're making a boil. I made them add fried hush puppies to the menu for you."

"Was this mission your idea or his?"

"His. But I'm a SEAL. So it's ours," Army replied. Jeff looked dubious as he transferred his narrowed gaze to Navy.

"How is now the right time for it?"

Navy answered easily. "If you weren't expecting it now, neither will they. We'll infiltrate, gather enough recon for a full extraction, then plan for that with complete intel and a complete team."

"And then you plan to try to locate this . . . Birdy character?"

Navy nodded. They hadn't told Rory yet, but TEAR had been at the farm. Cameras Army had installed there revealed a search party had ransacked it, activity that the three soldiers in the room had fully expected. But today they had learned that Birdy's father was messaging neighbors and friends looking for her, saying she'd been gone for two days without word. Navy didn't have concrete reasons to suspect TEAR was involved. His gut told him waiting for evidence would be stupid. They would infiltrate the compound where TEAR currently kept the donor farm, learn its security, then find AJ. If she was there, it would be quick and painless.

"All right. So recon, in and out, possibly a single extraction. No more?" At their agreement, he sighed and gave them both the final half shrug of assent: *I'm not your commanding officer, but you both respect me enough to treat me that way, so I'll respect you enough not to say you're dismissed.*

Army and Navy stood to leave, but Jeff said, "Navy, hang back."

Navy didn't sit again, but leaned against the side table in Jeff's office overlooking the rig, arms folded.

"I assume you're planning to tell Aurora about this friend of hers?"

"I'll inform Byron and Persy. They can tell—"

"Oh, don't be a damn coward," he spoke over the younger man. "It's obvious you two, I don't know, bonded. What happened?"

"I saved her life. She saved mine. Probably a couple times on each side." Navy reconsidered and added, "More saves of me on her scoreboard."

"And you're going to leave on this mission without telling her?"

Navy shrugged. "She doesn't want to speak to me. She can't trust me now."

Jeff hesitated before finally giving the telltale shrug again. "C'mon, there's snow crab tonight. If we don't get there first, Army won't leave a claw to suck on. Just . . . hell. You know I don't like to give advice."

"All evidence to the contrary."

"Don't be a fucking idiot, Nathan. That's all. Tell her how you feel."

Self-conscious about the shirt comment, Rory followed her mother's advice and left the empty lab to return to her small private room. She wasn't a fan of the tiny, dormitory-style spaces they currently were housed in, but she was grateful for her single room. The first few nights she had cried herself to sleep, reliving the days and weeks after her mother's death more vividly than ever. When that grief had faded, the pain of Navy's betrayal remained. She had nightmares of waking on the boat without him near, knowing everyone she loved was dead. Somehow a dream of being alone without him was a terror worse than the same dreams before she had met him.

Opening her door, she crossed to the sink and washed her face, then froze when she saw the black plastic shape on her desk. Her fiddle case. She crossed the room to open it and ran her fingers over the strings. Her father was making a gesture.

It was the right one. She could hear him telling her to bring it to the mess hall, entertain the rest of the team, relax and laugh for a night. Rory smiled, grabbed it, and headed for the mess.

Then she returned, changed her shirt—and jeans for good measure—and headed out again.

Byron watched over his hands folded on the base of the harmonica he played as his beautiful wife sang again to the accompaniment of his daughter's violin. He was glad the song didn't require much of him, as his throat was tight with emotion. He'd always believed he would see them together again, a family unit once more. But when a year, two, and then three had passed without news from Persy, he'd doubted her survival. For now, he shook off the persistent fear of being torn apart again by TEAR and enjoyed the moment he was in.

Persephone, always the best voice in the family, sang a playful melody of an ugly boy with a superior voice in a minor key, earning giggles from their audience when Rory emphasized the "ugly" with an off-key note from her strings.

Across the room, Byron observed that Navy was still watching Rory. It hadn't escaped the older man that Navy's usual intensity always seemed to soften when he was with her. Rory perceived herself betrayed by her stoic, scarred protector, but Byron would be forever grateful to him. Bits and pieces of their journey had been relayed to him secondhand, and he'd seen the healing wounds on both of them. He didn't ask, respecting the space she'd wanted from her father, but he sensed neither would be alive without the other one. And now that Rory was avoiding Navy, it hadn't escaped him how miserable they both were. *She fell in love with him*, Persy had insisted.

Watching Navy reveal a hint of a smile as the performer in question was finally smiling and laughing again, Byron held a different opinion. *He's in love with her.*

After enjoying a brief applause, Persy looked to her daughter and asked, "Can we sing our song?" Rory gave a nod, then glanced nervously at her father. He winked and played a brief snippet to remind her of the notes, and she hummed her bow over the strings to copy them once, poorly.

"I haven't played that since . . . I haven't played it in a while," she said quietly, excusing her rusty sound. "Give me a second."

Navy could feel the warmth from her cheeks already reddening and sensed her discomfort, but she took a deep breath, closed her eyes, and started to play. It was both an intro and a refresher she seemed to be playing, a sweet and plaintive tune. When she circled back and slowed it, Persephone took over with a soft southern curl to her voice, and during the chorus Rory sang quietly in backup.

Red lights are flashing on the highway
I wonder if we're gonna ever get home
I wonder if we're gonna ever get home tonight
Everywhere the water's getting rough
Your best intentions may not be enough
I wonder if we're gonna ever get home tonight.

But if you break down
I'll drive out and find you
If you forget my love
I'll try to remind you
And stay by you
When it don't come easy.

I don't know nothing except change will come
Year after year what we do is undone
Time keeps moving from a crawl to a run
I wonder if we're gonna ever get home.

You're out there walking down a highway
And all of the signs got blown away
Sometimes you wonder if you're walking in the wrong direction.

But if you break down
I'll drive out and find you
If you forget my love
I'll try to remind you
And stay by you
When it don't come easy.

Tears started to seep from Rory's eyes, though she didn't miss a note as she played through. Navy's hand tightened around the beer bottle he had been nursing all night. He hated to see her in more pain. Persephone's voice rose to a powerful crescendo, and several people rubbed goose bumps from their arms.

So many things that I had before
That don't matter to me now
Tonight I cry for the love that I've lost
And the love I've never found
When the last bird falls
And the last siren sounds
Someone will say what's been said before
It's only love we were looking for.

But if you break down
I'll drive out and find you
If you forget my love
I'll try to remind you
And stay by you
When it don't come easy.

Army and Navy passed a glance between them, both impressed with the song, the singer, the violinist. They clapped with the others while mother and daughter laughed and hugged through their tears.

"Maybe she'll finally get some sleep tonight," Army said with a good-natured smile and a swig of his beer.

"What do you mean?"

"My room's next to hers. Rory hasn't slept through a night since we arrived. Last week cryin' herself to sleep every night, this week I hear a scream every morning about three."

A few tables away, Rory hopped off her perch atop a chair back and announced she was wiped and heading for bed. Army met his friend's eyes and tipped his head knowingly.

As she put her violin away, Rory passed her father another smile.

"I like the applause a little more than the howling, don't you?" she teased.

"Oh, I don't know. I miss the chickens humming along."

Rory chuckled and gave him a warm hug, then kissed his cheek. "That was really sweet of you, Dad. Thank you for packing my fiddle."

Byron looked confused. "Sweetie. I'm loathe to admit this since you're speaking to me again, but I didn't bring it." He raised his eyebrows and looked over her head. She followed his glance and met Navy's eyes that she'd felt all night. She abruptly looked back to her father's shoulder.

"Good night." With a quick kiss to her mother's cheek, she disappeared.

CHAPTER 26

It was barely ten o'clock, but Navy stood outside her door in an empty hallway, unable to knock. All his training told him never to take on a mission without being completely prepared. He was not prepared for this. If she didn't let him in, didn't forgive him, he would leave tomorrow having hidden something from her again, and he wasn't prepared for the betrayal she would feel then.

You haven't been prepared for a fucking thing since you first met her, his brain countered. *She's had you off-balance since you fixed her jammed fingers.* And it had been the best time of his life. *Goddammit, man up.*

He reached up to knock.

Then he heard her scream. He grabbed the handle and cursed at the lock. Ten seconds later, the door shut behind him. She sat in the bed, arms folded over her knees, her head hanging, sobbing and sucking for breath.

"Rory." He reached the bed a second later and slid his hands over hers. At the moment she registered his weight on the bed, the warmth of his touch, she launched herself into his arms.

"Navy. You were dead. Everybody was dead . . . you were dead, and I was on the boat, and you weren't there anymore, and I was alone."

His arms crashed around her slim form, drawing her shaking body to him. "Shhh, baby. I'm here, Rory. I've got you." Navy felt the wave of relief, of rightness wash through him as she slowly stopped sobbing and caught her breath, but he didn't move an inch.

"I missed you so much."

Navy worried he might crush her when his arms tightened reflexively. "God, I've missed you, Rory."

"How . . . how are you in here?"

"I was at the door."

Rory leaned back enough to see his face in the dark. "It's locked." She saw the shadow of a smile.

"I've got skills." Touching her face, he closed the inches between them and kissed her softly, then leaned his forehead against hers. "I'm sorry, Rory. I hated hiding anything from you."

"I realized tonight . . . if you'd told me my mother was alive, I probably would have trusted you less."

"Do you trust me?"

Rory kissed him. "Yes. I can't help it." Then she kissed him again, wrapping her body around him as he pressed her into the pillows.

She woke in his arms and, like their few mornings on the boat, she watched him sleeping again in the pale morning light that her tiny window permitted. She hadn't forgotten how his body was shaped and felt, but she had underestimated how much she craved his closeness. Rory wondered if there would be a day when they could live a normal life together, not under threat of discovery, not desperate to solve the world's post-antibiotic crisis. Not burdened with the memory of people he'd given to TEAR, a guilt she knew darkened his face more than his deep blue marks. She feared she was the answer to her own questions. If she could solve it, they could give the cure to everyone. They could expose TEAR. They could return those poor people to their families. They could live somewhere other than this man-made island. She felt no closer to that elusive answer than she had back in Woods Hole.

"You're staring at me, Rory. What are you thinking?" he spoke without opening his eyes.

"How do you do that?" she asked in amazement. "I would have sworn you were sleeping."

"I keep telling you. I have skills." Opening his eyes, he kissed her forehead.

She answered his original question. "I was thinking about how to solve the mystery of my resistance. My resistance to resistant bacteria. If I could do it, maybe life could be normal for us. For everyone here."

He leaned up on an arm, studying her face. "Have you made any progress in the lab? Jeff tells me everyone really respects you there."

She shrugged and sighed. "I feel like something's in my grasp, but the lab equipment analyzing the genetic side of things keeps giving us lots of noise. I need a better lab, I suppose."

"I know Jeff didn't spare any expense there, but if you need something, you should ask him. He's willing to do anything to help the researchers." Navy toyed with her fingers, bringing them to his mouth to kiss.

"What's his motivation here? I know you told me a little about his background. Emile in the lab said his wife died of an infection, but it sounded like rumor."

Navy nodded. "It's true. He's only told me the story once, when he was deep into a very expensive bottle of whiskey on their anniversary. It was . . . it was awful. She died slowly, painfully. By the time she passed away, over a dozen surgeries had left her a quadruple amputee. She begged him to help her die. I don't know if he did, but I can tell you he doesn't like to speak of it. And if you help solve this problem, he'll make sure it's available to the whole world." Navy watched her try to hide her suspicions with little success.

Faced with his knowing expression, Rory gave in. "I was worried about that. If he became so rich from his businesses, I feared he would try to patent something and make himself richer. I know that assumes I'll get over these hurdles, but . . . I followed you because you assured me this team was trying to help *everyone*."

Navy kissed her forehead. "I know you didn't follow me because you trusted me right then. I've worked with Jeff for three years now. If you solve this, he'll make sure no one has to pay for your cure. And he'll make sure you never have to worry for money, either." Navy glanced at his watch and then met her blue-green eyes again. "Now it's time for a conversation I didn't want to have. But I want you to trust me."

Her anxiety for what was to follow was all over her as she sat up in the bed. "You're going, aren't you? You're going after TEAR."

Navy's response didn't reassure her. "I'm going after the people I hurt. The people I stole from their lives and families. I may not get them this time, but I plan to find where they are. Returning them all to their families will be a bigger mission."

"So, you and Army? Just—what? Recon?"

He smiled tenderly at her use of unfamiliar military jargon. "Basically, yes. I know where they were, and I think I know where they were moved in the last year. But . . . that's not all I need to tell you. Yesterday, we learned that AJ—Birdy—her father is looking for her. She's gone missing for three days."

Rory's face drained of all color and she gripped his hand. "What? Birdy's missing?"

"I wanted to tell you yesterday, but . . ." he shook his head. "I couldn't ruin the first night I saw you speaking to your dad again. Army and I are going to find her. We're going to try to bring her here." The conviction in his voice didn't seem to lessen her fears.

Rory turned and leaned her face into her hands. "I did this. I put her in harm's way." She shook her head, the guilt overwhelming. Her closest friend, now in the grasp of the very people they had been trying to evade. "What a coward's way. I traded my safety for hers."

"You didn't, and you saved her life. We both know that infection would have killed her."

"I'm going with you."

"No."

"Don't act like I didn't save your ass several times on the last mission."

He chuckled. "Thank you. But still no. This isn't something you have any training for, and I've had my fill of seeing you in danger. Your training is needed here." He lifted her face to his. "Hey, AJ's on my team now, and Army and I never leave a team member behind. We will get her back."

CHAPTER 27

A storm was blowing in from the north when the helicopter lifted off, Army at the controls. Rory held Navy's eyes through the window before it banked, turned away east, and flew toward the mainland. She reminded herself what he'd told her as they got dressed and said their goodbyes that morning: *In a week or two, we'll be back here with AJ, eating lobster and crab and celebrating Christmas. And you'll solve this.*

She hoped he was right. For now, they all huddled against the cold spray of an angry ocean and headed back indoors to the lab. The team there was anxious to review new lab reports from the mice they had injected with antibodies isolated from Rory's blood serum.

Settling down at a conference table with the small group of scientists, her mind on AJ's whereabouts, she mused that she was in a room full of the smartest people in the world for *this* particular problem. Navy was right, she was needed here and should focus on this problem if she wanted the government to stop hunting them. If they couldn't solve it together, no one could.

Emile, the molecular biochemist, was working on nanoparticles that could defeat some resistant bacterial defense mechanisms. Petre, a Georgian virologist, still felt strongly that bacteriophages could be trained to deliver gene therapies that disabled the bacterial genes causing antibiotic resistance, restoring efficacy to medicines long thought useless. Veronica was from Seattle and had a doctorate in microbial genetics, and had completed brilliant work that might identify new human gene therapies to aid in natural human immune response. And Rory's mother, who had worked in each of these fields, was the thread that helped weave their findings together in hopes of a powerful tool that could do everything. Everything that Rory's body had figured out, but wasn't revealing.

"So the murine experiments are improving?" Persy prompted Veronica, who nodded eagerly.

Rory, seated next to her father, whispered, "*Murine* means mouse."

"I knew that," he deadpanned back.

"Yes, for the first time, they are exhibiting success with the antibodies we're terming *Ror alpha, Ror beta,* etc., through *Ror lambda*. Compared to the prior batch we drew from Rory's blood sample, which was more refined and possibly excluded certain antibodies unexpectedly, test-subject survival is currently at ninety-nine percent."

"So up from fifty-seven percent last round? That's good," Persy nodded.

"And nice to hear some of those poor mice are surviving," Jeff joked. "Your lab rat budget was getting scary."

Persy looked to Emile.

Emile cleared his throat. "On the topic of cell-wall targeting, bad news. Unchanged from last week—I've had acceptable levels of success with seven of our twelve target pathogens that caused the most deaths during the die-off, but they continue to mutate. They are growing and changing, evolving faster than we can develop a molecule that will defeat them."

Rory leaned close to her father again. "Emile is the one building the microscopic-sized structures from carbon molecules that can punch through bacteria's walls, but he's seen it work a little differently in different types of bacteria. They're learning," she whispered.

"Are you still receiving a good supply of samples from our contacts?" Jeff interrupted from the corner. A crucial tenet of their research, required by the billionaire, was to always be testing current samples of bacteria isolated from patients worldwide. If they worked in a bubble, Jeff theorized, final results might still fall short of what the world needed now. Bacteria mutated too often to assume that the strains they kept growing for their research were a true model of the real world.

"Yes, we are," Emile confirmed. "And the mutations are in those strains, too. It makes sense—we're looking at both Gram-positives and Gram-negatives, aerobic and anaerobic—so I guess they've sub-adapted considerably. My team is also mapping the samples we're receiving into Rory's database, and we may soon be learning more from that data."

"So the cell wall still seems to be the issue, correct?" Persy asked.

"Right," Emile agreed. "We know the resistance gene gave bacteria an enhanced cell wall defense mechanism against antibiotics, but we're still trying to understand the nuances cropping up now between species. We're using both molecular pairing techniques and gene sequencing, to see if there's something changed in their genes that we could work on."

"Ah—that reminds me. Where are we on sequencing Rory's genes?"

"I can answer—I took that over from Veronica," Rory spoke up. "It's still a little sketchy, and I've got a lot of noise in the data that isn't just epigenetic variations." Referring to the DNA sequences that were once thought to be useless, then discovered about half a century earlier to govern the expression of other neighboring genes, Rory meant that her own DNA was coming through the sequencer with genes no computers or databases could recognize. "There's nothing in existing libraries to match the gene sequences that are showing up in the data. I'm left wondering if it's me—literally, my DNA—or the DNA sequencing equipment. Or, of course, user error."

"That's my first culprit," Petre laughed. "Send me what you're seeing, and I'll try to help."

"Thanks," Rory said with a grateful smile, "I will. Fortunately, I keep seeing the same apparent errors. So there's consistency."

"Well, let's have Petre check your methods. Garbage in, garbage out, you know," Persy advised. The age-old computer science adage warned that data and research performed or gathered without exact methods would always yield inexact, or garbage, results.

Petre gave a sigh. "Well, since I'm last in this lineup, you should know my results are looking worse."

"Specificity?" Persy guessed. Rory sensed Petre's dejection at being the champion of a treatment method that wasn't very popular. The history of using bacteriophages, or phages for short, to treat bacterial infections was a long and winding one, fraught with research that had been validated as often as it had been debunked. Rory had studied the research topic in the past, and more recently refreshed herself, but Petre himself was a walking textbook of how to use the viruses that preyed on bacteria to hunt down bacteria in the human body. He gave Persy an update, a confirmation of the problem she had known—that the bacteriophages themselves had preferences for specific bacteria. Matching the bacteriophage strain to the bacterial strain you wanted to target was difficult enough, but keeping the virus active and viable and getting it into the patient was another world of challenges. Viruses were often unstable, requiring a live cell culture to "inhabit" to avoid their degradation into useless bits of protein and genetic material. Delivery in itself was a key component to the success of any treatment. If drugs were likely to make it to patients all over the world with success, then they had to be easy to deliver, from how they were swallowed or injected, all the way up to what refrigeration, if any, would be required to maintain their efficacy after shipping. And Petre was still stuck on an obstacle miles ahead of those issues.

"I feel like I'm hearing the same conversations happening every week," Jeff spoke up at a lull in the conversation between Persy and Petre. He leaned forward on his knees and looked them each in the eye. "I told you guys when we started this, we needed to break the mold of what traditional thoughts and approaches have been brought to this problem. It's why I brought you all together, because your research was brilliant. I need you guys to try harder here. Rory—do you mind if I share the story of your friend?"

Rory shook her head. "Go ahead."

"Rory's friend AJ is missing. We believe she's been captured by

TEAR because Rory knew she had a serious infection and gave her a transfusion. Everyone here knows the transfusion must have worked, because almost a month later, she's still alive. In theory, this young woman is now a new clue for *their* research teams to solve this before we do."

Silence filled the room until Veronica voiced confusion.

"Jeff, I'm not trying to undermine your motivations for us, we appreciate them. But . . . that doesn't make scientific sense. Rory's antibodies shouldn't be present in her friend's bloodstream still. They naturally break down."

"Reassuring yourself with 'shoulds' is a pretty shitty way to do this research. In fact, that word might just get outlawed around here. If anyone had ever done what they *should have* for the past sixty years and stopped abusing antibiotics, we wouldn't all have buried several of our loved ones. If you go around assuming that everything will behave the way it should, you won't be making any new history." The fury in Jeff's voice was tempered only out of respect for the individuals assembled.

Rory stood and walked to the window, her mind whirling with that itchy feeling that she knew something her brain wouldn't translate. But AJ and Navy were filling her mind, too.

"You're right," Persy agreed. "And let's try to quit using that mindset. But Veronica is also right, Jeffrey. Rory's antibodies are only helpful for a short period in the recipients."

"Quit fucking assuming! Rory is an anomaly. She's evolved something no one else has."

"Well, technically that's wrong, too," Emile said quietly, and Jeff's blazing eyes pinned him down. He shrugged, daunted but righteous. "Evolution happens at a population level, over millennia. We can't see it here in one person, only the results of it."

"You're goddamned right about one thing: you can't see. You need to quit trying to see things as you always have!" Jeff shouted. The room fell silent as Jeff stood and paced to the windows.

"Strong convictions, weakly held," Byron said quietly. All eyes looked to him.

Byron stood now, too, and made a gesture with open hands that seemed to acknowledge everyone's points of view.

"Evolution happens everywhere there is an environmental pressure. Either a species survives that pressure or is killed by it. Yes, humanity is currently on the losing end of that story, and yes, we are all here doing our best to reverse that. Let's agree for the moment that Rory's body has an adaptation we don't yet fully understand and we all generally agree is beneficial to her own survival. Hopefully to all of ours as well. What I think we all need to do is take a break, return to work, and remember that a bias toward what we have always known is very natural, very human. It also slows the process of discovery. We need to use what we know, but we also need to be open to learning something we don't already know. We need to have strong convictions that are weakly held."

Everyone nodded throughout the room, a few repeating it to themselves quietly. Persy called an end to the meeting, and Emile, Veronica, and Petre left. Rory stayed where she was, leaning against a low cabinet with her arms crossed over her chest.

"Well done," Jeff told Byron. "Sorry I—"

"Don't be," Persy interrupted him. "They needed it. We all do. The only bias here should be a bias toward action."

PART FOUR

Trees Uptorn

CHAPTER 28

Outside Woodstock, Virginia

Towering pines of the Shenandoah National Forest surrounded Navy and Army as they hiked toward the location of the compound where they suspected survivors were being kept. Their intel showed that a decent number of people commuted to the site daily, and the majority were more qualified to work in a hospital. But their suspicions were confirmed when one of Jeff's computer "analysts," as they were politely termed—actually hackers with access to the most sophisticated surveillance tools Army had ever had the pleasure of playing with—reported a biomedical waste incinerator was on the property. Only the presence of active research and living patients would necessitate a regular stream of biomedical waste.

"All right, let's go over this again—high level," Navy said. "Plan A: surveillance for sufficient confirmation that this is our place. Infiltrate when we know enough about the security setup. Install cameras. Find AJ. Extract AJ, hike back to the heli, go home, have a beer, and plan for Phase 2." In Phase 2, they would extract every donor and return them all to their families.

Army typically would have picked up where he'd left off and explored the contingency plans they'd rehearsed in case of Plan A going off script.

"Can we talk about Plan F?" Army asked instead. Navy sent him a wry grin. Plan F was their private code for *fuckered*, or what to do if everything went wrong.

"Always have to," Navy nodded.

"Yeah, but I keep thinking . . . if we took Plan A and stopped at installing bugs, then camped here for a few days while Jeff organized reinforcements, we could storm the castle and rescue all the fair maidens at once."

"If the security isn't extreme."

"You've seen the satellite images. There's nothing to indicate that they've militarized this place other than fencing and a gate with a couple guards." Army pressed a point he'd made several times before. "Once AJ is extracted, they'll move this compound again like they did after Persephone freed you and me." Persephone had found them when her own curiosity had led her through the maze of paperwork and military stonewalling that prevented most TEAR researchers from knowing where their donor blood samples originated.

Only her own suspicions—and fears that the truth might be worse than those suspicions—had driven her to keep digging until she found how and where the "donor farm" was really conducted. Over thirty individuals, ranging from children to middle-aged patients, were being held in a nondescript building outside of Alexandria, Virginia. A team of medical professionals kept them in induced comas, hidden from their families, unconscious to and unknown by the world. Navy and Army had been at the same facility, though they were being used as lab rats instead of a source of blood antibodies to test. Dr. Rajni had proceeded to human trials without Persephone's agreement, and their SEAL team had been among the second round of "volunteers"—the first had all died, as had every member of their team save the two of them. When Persephone discovered it and argued with Rajni that volunteers didn't need to be chained to gurneys, Rajni had begged her to let the trial continue, convinced that Army and Navy would survive.

Persephone agreed to keep it quiet, but she had returned late that night and released them both. When Rajni discovered it, he and Persephone had argued bitterly, but he'd agreed to cover it up. At that point, all three of them knew it was time for them to die, at least publicly. Persephone contacted Jeff, who had reached out in the past to entice her to join a pharmaceutical company he owned. She begged him to help them all. With that call, the Resistance was born.

Army pressed, "Once they move it a third time, we might never

find it again. We should do this thing right, do it now, do it once."
He advocated for a complete takedown of the donor farm and recovery of every person he and Navy had themselves helped to en-
slave.

"You hiding a Ranger team in your pocket?"

Army chuckled. "Those pansies?" Then he sobered, stopped
and turned to his oldest friend. "Seriously, brother. We could find
people. Jeff has the connections—soldiers who retired and went
into private firms. International teams, too."

Navy shook his head. "We risk exposing the whole Resistance
before there's a cure to offer. The military would just tell the public
that they were trying to save everyone. Sacrifice a few to reach the
greater goal. No one will ever believe us that they're trying to
commercialize a cure and control who gets it."

Army shrugged. "By that logic, the only way to really expose
them would be to give them the cure, watch them try to control it,
and then tell the world we have it, too, and everyone's getting it for
free. Every person who tricked us into robbing families of their
loved ones—every last fucking one of them—they'll never be punished."

Frustrated, Navy turned and kept hiking, knowing Army was
right. But right now, Plan F was still too fuckered to work.

CHAPTER 29

Hibernia Wind and Energy Farm

"So we followed every step correctly . . . I don't get it." Petre rubbed the bridge of his long aquiline nose, and his glasses wobbled loose before he caught them and shoved them back. They sat in Rory's lab comparing her prior results with their new attempt together. He kept rereading Rory's DNA sequence results after running the test for her, hoping for something to jump out at him. Science was, in itself, messier than any researcher wanted to admit; samples could get tainted with a stray bit of DNA from another person, from bacteria, even from a speck of lab rat dandruff. Imperfection wasn't unusual, it was expected, but if they followed the steps again and again until they finally got it right, eventually they would be sure to see a new, sensible result.

Rory's, however, were consistently wrong, as if her DNA sample were being corrupted the same exact way every time. Having Petre run the sample should have eliminated that possibility.

"Yes, and if it were genetic sequences that made sense, that matched up with any other human library known out there, it wouldn't be a big deal. I could entertain the idea that I'm carrying some unique mutations. Hell, that would be great news. But this isn't in any database. I've even run it against primate databases. I can't see it being anything but an error," Rory reasoned. "Maybe we need to get a technician to check the equipment?"

Petre leaned back in his chair, arms crossed, and stared up at the ceiling. "Well, like your father said, it could be a mutation we haven't seen before. It would be unusual, but still—let's think without bias, right?"

Rory hitched herself up onto a countertop and gave a dry laugh. "You know, if you upend all your assumptions . . . then logic would follow that the government researchers have already solved this. We are probably laboring under an assumption that they haven't found the answer."

"Couldn't it also imply we've found it, but don't know yet?" Petre asked, puzzled.

Rory nodded. "I've actually had that feeling for weeks. Like it's just within my grasp. Up here." She tapped her forehead.

Petre smiled. "My mother was a brilliant physicist. She believed that all ideas are already conceived, just waiting in a dormant state for some moment of revelation. She was very spiritual. To her, ideas were the only things that were timeless, and our bodies, our brains, were just their vessels. Like, you know, the mitochondrion?"

Rory tipped her head, considering it. The mitochondrion was considered the powerhouse of the cells of multicellular organisms, because it took in nutrients and broke them down for human cells to use. Single-celled bacteria didn't have mitochondria. Mitochondria had its own DNA, termed *mtDNA*, and current scientific thinking posited that mitochondria were once, long ago when life on Earth was new, separate bacteria that evolved to be an integral part of the complex cells as we knew them now, performing a function for the cell and receiving protection within it.

She looked up at Petre as both their expressions changed from confusion to a dawning new idea.

"Do you think this is mitochondrial DNA?" she asked, and at the same time he said, "Did you check mtDNA databases?" They both rushed to their computer stations and ran the analysis, but it didn't take long to disprove their theory. None of the nonsense sequences in Rory's DNA matched current databases of mtDNA, which hadn't changed in millennia.

"Dormant . . . dormant . . ." Rory repeated to herself. *Figure it out, for fuck's sake!* she wanted to scream.

Her wrist phone, the new one Jeff had issued her when she arrived, buzzed against her skin. She turned her wrist up. Navy was messaging. The light illuminated her forearm, projecting the message across her skin: *Last transition, all comms going off soon. I love you. Should have said it in person.*

When her hand came to her mouth with a silent gasp, Petre sensed she might like some privacy and excused himself. She messaged back: *I love you. I should have, too. Please be safe.*

Then he replied: *Don't worry. I took the fish-blood oath. I've got your strength.*

She thought of their night and morning, and her blood warmed at the recollection of his strong body touching hers. She didn't want to correct him that, scientifically speaking, he wouldn't still have her antibodies in his bloodstream. He meant it in a more poetic sense.

Rory froze then, her eyes rising but seeing nothing in the room as a memory fresh from their morning crystallized in her brain. Navy had been standing beside the bed as she lay smiling up at him, watching him dress. The memory overlaid that of the time at the hospital when he lay on the gurney and she stitched closed his wound, too shy to remove his pants so she could do a better job, but curious if the blue marks went beyond his waistband.

This morning's memory was different. The blue marks had started above his navel.

They had shifted. Lightened, too, across his chest. As if they were changing, disappearing, turning off.

No, you idiot. It's the reverse. Something turned on, something altered. Activated.

She didn't yet understand, but she knew she would soon. She texted him urgently: *Wait, don't turn off comms. Don't do anything. Wait for my next message.*

"Petre!" she shouted, and then she screamed it.

CHAPTER 30

Outside Woodstock, Virginia

At their camp on the backside of a low bluff that gave them a vantage point into the compound, Navy sat across from Army as both men waited impatiently for his wrist phone to message again. Finally it buzzed, and he frowned curiously.

"She's asking if I have the ability to do a hologram video communication. Is that going to set off alerts?" Navy asked.

Army reasoned, "I just don't think they know yet that they should be listening around here to cell communications. I would bet it's all right. But it resets our clock—I still want a full twenty-four-hour quiet period before we try to head in." As their comms expert, he believed strongly in electronic silence as key to a surprise attack. Analysts who were assigned to surveil for activity as a defensive measure got bored quickly, and that was when Army felt it was best to move—when those watchers had distracted themselves.

They set up a holo-pad and connected back to Rory's station at the rig, and her face filled the screen with Jeff, Petre, Byron, and Persephone in the visible background.

"What's going on?" Navy started.

"I think we've figured it out. You messaged me about the fish-blood oath, and I was thinking about things and I remembered this morning—anyway," she halted, blushing furiously. "Look under your shirt. Look at the marks. They've changed."

Surprised, Navy glanced down, pulling open his jacket and dragging up his shirt. The move revealed abdominal muscles that were marked with blue, but far less than a few weeks ago. He hadn't even noticed.

"We've been trying to figure out how my DNA sequences are full of all this nonsense, and we can't match them to any human genetic sequences. Petre crossed-checked them against his phage libraries and they match! They lie dormant, embedded into the code until—"

"Rory, wait. I don't understand. Tell me simply."

She took a long breath. "I realized if your marks were changing, something had to have been activated, something that was embedded in your cells and lying dormant until I gave you a transfusion. I think whatever they gave you years ago was a bacteriophage and that it embedded into your genetic sequences, where it waits for signs of bacterial infection. I guess the sepsis you contracted re-vived it, or I revived it, too. My DNA has the DNA of viruses in it, viruses that are hiding out in a safe place and becoming part of our cells, part of our immune systems! They are viruses that kill bacteria. We did it, Navy. We have the cure!"

Navy was too stunned to answer. "I . . . I don't get it. It's been with me all along?"

"Yes! And you too, Army. We have more work to do, but I guarantee you some of those survivors in my database and at the compound there—they must have evolved or acquired the same viral embedded protection. I've got to get there and get blood sam-ples to be sure, but—"

"You're not coming here, Rory."

"Plan F," Army intoned cheerfully.

Jeff perked up. "Plan F? Why?"

Rory looked over her shoulder at him, stumped.

Army replied, "It's the best bet. Clean sweep, full takeover. Hopefully not too hostile."

"It's dangerous. We don't know enough." Navy shook his head, his eyes on Rory's.

"So we'll work here until we do while Jeff sends in backup."

"I can work on backup," Jeff nodded.

"Hey! I explained my concept. Now what the hell are you guys talking about?" Rory interrupted.

Army seemed concerned suddenly, looking through the screen projection of her at something else. He crossed in back of its camera, out of sight. They heard him say, "Comms off."

Suddenly the screen went black, and Navy's face and a backdrop of forest disappeared from Rory's holo-laptop screen. She spun to look at Jeff questioningly. He shrugged.

"They were talking about bringing in more support and having a full team storm the compound."

"What happened? Why did it drop off?" She tried to call them again and got no connection, then tried twice more as panic gnawed at her throat.

Jeff started for the door.

"I'm calling in reinforcements."

CHAPTER 31

Hibernia Wind and Energy Farm

Rory returned to the lab and tried to focus. She needed to work on building experiments that could confirm their theories about her DNA. She and Petre proposed to the research team that the fastest method would be to introduce her blood to an infectious bacteria in vitro, strictly in the lab setting, and see if they could prove bacteriophage activity happening. If that result was positive, meaning her cells had made bacteriophage viruses as an immune response, then they would attempt to translate it into a mouse model. To achieve that, they would provide one set of mice a gene therapy to impart the same ability to make bacteriophages within their own cells. Another control set of mice would not be given the gene, but both would then be injected with bacteria. The results—meaning which survived the infections—would be a strong indicator of whether their theory was right.

When the teams split to get to work on constructing the experiments, Rory was left to herself and her worries. She sought out Jeff, and found him, Byron, Persephone, and their computer analysts in a meeting. A large table was flanked by about ten different computer screens that all seemed to be tasked with different efforts. The analysts kept their backs to the table but periodically turned to quietly report something.

"Can I join you?" she asked as she walked in and took a seat, intending to stay regardless of their answer.

"Sure," Jeff nodded. "We're working on this from a couple

angles. I've reached out to private military groups with black-ops experience I can hire to get to the compound Navy and Army targeted and provide backup as needed, and get an extra helicopter here with them."

"Honey, you need to know—if this cure works, we have a lot of decisions to make about how to announce it and take down TEAR for once and for all," Persephone explained to Rory with a motherly hand covering hers. "I know you're worried about Navy, but he's a pretty tough guy."

Rory looked to Jeff. "What do you think? Are they okay?"

Jeff made the facial equivalent of a shrug. "I agree with Persephone—there's nothing they can't handle, and I don't think the compound was heavily fortified. We're trying to get access to today's satellite images now and comb through them for anything that tells us more about why Army called for communications silence."

"Navy told me that the guy in charge of TEAR, Kessler . . . he's dangerous, manipulative. What more do you actually know about him? He knew Navy and Army personally and tried to have them killed. Wouldn't he try again if he found out they were alive?" Rory asked.

Jeff glanced at Persy, who nodded her assent.

"We worried along the same lines," he said. "Before Persephone left TEAR and feigned death, she had reason to believe that Navy and Army and their team weren't the only people used as human test subjects."

"Jason Rajni admitted as much to me," Persy told her daughter. "That was when we knew that if I didn't fake my death and try to do research elsewhere, more people would be in danger."

Byron asked, "How much does the government know about the human trials? About the deaths?"

"Nothing, I think. I suspect that Kessler bullied Rajni into it because so much money had already been spent on research that he needed something to show for it. Even one patient surviving would have been news to share and keep the cash flowing in until a real cure could be found." Persy shuddered as she remembered Kessler.

"Kessler was a snake, the kind who charmed his way up the congressional ladder and only aspired to more power."

"So what's next?" Rory asked. "I want to go with your teams to the compound."

They all responded simultaneously: "No." "That's not happening." "Hell, no."

"Oh, give me a break. I'm not going to play SEAL team six. I'll wait until it's safe and then help with the survivors." She rolled her eyes and announced, "I'm going."

Jeff raised a hand to both of her parents. "Let me just disabuse you of this notion, Aurora. If Army and Navy and even my teams were to be met with a full military contingent—something Kessler is perfectly capable of—you'd be the perfect bargaining chip. But only if you're here, where they can't find you."

Byron leaned across the table and slammed down a fist, and the analysts all jumped a little in surprise. "My daughter isn't your fucking bargaining chip." His eyes blazed at Jeff, who looked respectfully bemused.

"I wouldn't play that hand unless I absolutely had to, to save our team. Even then, Kessler wouldn't touch her. We already have the upper hand if Rory's theory proves out—and all we would need is to buy more time to prove it." He pointed a finger at Rory. "Which is why you're staying right here and proving it. It took you only three weeks to solve the puzzle we've been stumped by for three years. You're not going anywhere near what could become a war zone."

Mollified, Byron leaned back in his chair and crossed his arms, but he couldn't resist lobbing an arrow across the bow. "So tell me this, brilliant tech billionaire: Why do you have only one helicopter?"

Jeff let out a sigh. "That's a fair point."

CHAPTER 32

Outside Woodstock, Virginia

"You know I'm right. It'd be much more pleasant to go through this if you'd just admit that." Sitting on a fallen log at their campsite, he watched Navy sharpen his knife as they waited for dusk.

Navy grunted in reply and kept sharpening.

"Look, I won't tell anyone you got captured."

"You're damned right you won't. This is not a capture."

"That's right. It's just a strategic surrender."

The knife thudded into the log beside Army's thigh.

"Fair point," Army agreed. "Look, I know I'm right. If there was any chance, any, that they heard Rory's transmission, they've got a massive leg up, and we need to both distract them and take down this whole compound."

Navy sighed. "I get it. Comms off, Rory and the team are safe, and Jeff is probably already recruiting for Plan F. So I'll let them catch me, you sneak in behind, and we can get the lay of the land inside the compound easily." But *easily* implied they knew what they were getting into. *Easily* implied they had a clear idea of the force ratio. Two to twenty? They were SEALs. With their skill set and experience, that ratio seemed manageable. But two to fifty? And how well trained was this particular set of guards?

"Exactly. Take control without bruises. Kessler will never feel like such a fuckup as when he finds out." Army said it holding Navy's eyes. *We've been here before and survived, brother,* he was saying. Navy nodded and stood as they shouldered their packs and started for the compound. They hiked down toward the exterior fence, closer toward the gate, then crouched down out of sight to watch the guards prepare for evening shift change.

Hibernia Wind and Energy Farm

Veronica pushed her short-bobbed hair back behind her ear again as she leaned down to look at her microscope's digital display. On the small screen that relayed the digital representation of the happenings five hundred times smaller than human eyes could detect, bacteria interacted with Rory's blood on a scale that older, simpler microscopes could not relay. As light technology and digital displays had evolved, the marriage of them allowed microbiologists and nanotechnologists like Veronica to visualize progress at a nearly atom-by-atom level.

So far, they had tried to create in vitro—essentially in their test tubes—an approximation of what would happen in Rory's bloodstream should she have caught a significant infection. So far today, they had not seen progress. Rory was still certain that she was right, but Veronica was ready to call it a day.

"I want dinner and a glass of wine, and I'll review the video of everything tomorrow," she finally said, and confirmed the digital display was not only monitoring but recording.

"Go ahead," Rory nodded. "Thanks for all the hard work today. I know I demanded a massive experiment to be set up in record time."

"It's cool." Veronica waved a hand. "Eureka moments are truly exciting. In fact, kind of exhausting. Let's sleep and get ready for another one tomorrow over coffee, eh?" She gave the younger woman a warm wink, but Rory shook her head.

"I'm just not that hungry, thanks. I'll stay and watch the paint dry a little longer." She nodded to the screen of her holo-laptop, which mirrored Veronica's display.

Veronica gave her a last wave goodnight and disappeared, and Rory indulged in a final attempt to connect to Navy. *Message not received* came back for the fiftieth time that day. She watched the blinking display and sighed.

She wanted to understand what might be happening at TEAR's command, but her ignorance of its structure and research progress stifled her hope of even imagining. So, as with any problem, it was best to start with what she did know. *So what do we know?* she thought. First, that TEAR was being led by a man who knew little about science, a lot about war, and aspired to greater power. Second, that TEAR was capable of testing dangerous, half-baked treatments on unwilling human subjects. Third, that their cure, if proven effective, could be in the DNA of a whole lot of people out there whose cells had also become the willing hosts for beneficial viruses that were deadly to bacteria.

And fourth, that the list of those people existed on a database that Rory had developed. Now that she knew how dangerous TEAR was, she wished she had never created it.

The list of things she didn't know was too long to explore, but Navy's status of alive, dead, or captured dominated her concerns. She thought of her mother's story, wondered if this was how her mother had felt when she decided to leave TEAR and fake her own death. Not knowing whether you could protect someone you loved, if they were safe . . . Rory stopped herself going down that path as her eyes swam with unshed tears.

Through the mists in her vision, living cells teemed on the screen before her, bacterial and human cells mixing together as the bacterial cells frequently multiplied or moved and the human cells sat stuck without the benefit of a heart to push them somewhere useful.

She wiped her eyes as a movement smaller than both cells happened along the boundary of a red blood cell. Blinking away tears, she leaned in close.

At the cell wall of a red blood cell, a tiny stream of little simple structures began to march out. Viruses. They had an upper shape like a top that a child could spin, pointed on both ends: the capsid. From one end of the capsid, a tiny cylinder extended, and from that cylinder, six leg-like projections were attached. The nano-sized army floated in the plasma between her cells, and each time a virus that her cells had birthed encountered a bacterium, it latched on instantly with all six legs. The cylinder would lower to the bacterial cell wall and begin to drill through it, then transfer its genetic code over to the bacterium.

Rory watched, riveted, as the bacteriophage viruses slowly invaded every bacterial cell in the screen view, and then the bacterial cells, within an hour, began one by one to burst open, or lyse, like little water balloons rupturing in slow motion.

"Eureka," she whispered to an empty room. The next phase of testing could start as early as tomorrow or the next day in the mouse model. For Rory, her theory was already fully proven. No good scientist would accept the results of a single test, but she had just watched it happen live on screen, and she knew in her gut that it would work on a larger scale—they would simply have to develop a gene therapy that imparted to everyone the same genetic advantage that she had. And her database would help.

If TEAR doesn't get to them first.

She walked directly to the room where the analysts worked and politely asked the one named Kurt to tell her everything they knew about Kessler, the compound, and TEAR.

"I'm worried about Navy. It just makes me feel better to have information."

"Um . . . sure. I mean, we have files on them all you can read through. Here, let me show you. See, there's kind of a dossier on all of the players we really know about—Kessler, his reporting officers, the key researchers at TEAR." He opened up computer files on Kessler and let her peruse. "That Kessler, he seems like a real prick. My research shows he's never had a social media account in his life."

Rory found that worthy of a chuckle. "And that's what upset you about him?"

Kurt shook his head in slow, dramatic fashion. "It's sick, man. It's pathological."

"Well, you've got a lot about him anyway. You even have his medications and allergies," she mused as she scanned the info.

Kurt nodded. "Well, that balances it out. At least that psycho can't enjoy shellfish."

Rory glanced at him, afraid to reveal too much. He seemed oblivious to her plan, but she thought of Navy saying she didn't have the skills for deception.

"Show me what TEAR looks like. What their security looks like."

Outside Woodstock, Virginia

"You know, I thought we had done demoralizing things in our time together," Navy grumbled. From many yards away, his partner chuckled into the tiny earpiece Navy wore. His position near the gate's guard station was chosen so that he would be seen, intercepted, and intentionally captured, yet no one had noticed him even during shift change. "A rent-a-cop would have found me by now."

"A blind rent-a-cop," Army laughed in his ear. "We could be here all night if you don't do something."

"If you ever tell anyone about this . . ." Navy began to belly-crawl toward the gate entrance.

"Oh, I'll be telling our grandchildren about this. Weekly."

"Now we're both having children, eh? Got your eye on somebody?"

"We're about to save her, actually. Don't steal my thunder and act the hero when it's my turn."

Now Navy stifled a laugh. At the gatehouse, he decided to at least make it fun for himself, and jumped up to surprise the guard. The young soldier startled, trying to engage his rifle.

"Safety's on," Navy hinted. As expected, the guard sounded the alarm and three more guards hurtled out the entry doors, guns at the ready. "Oh, shoot. I didn't realize there would be so many of you. Darn." As he let himself be cuffed and dragged inside, he glanced over his shoulder and saw Army easily dodge inside the compound gate, roll to the shadows, and reposition himself to follow them in.

CHAPTER 33

Hibernia Wind and Energy Farm

Her mind resolved, Rory threw a few items into the pockets of her jacket and snuck down to the boat launch. The catamaran sat suspended in a dock lift. No one but she could do this, the ultimate bargaining chip. She would get the boat close to Nova Scotia, far enough from the Hibernia that, when her wrist phone connected to TEAR headquarters, they wouldn't suspect the rig's role in the Resistance. It took her a few minutes to determine how to lower the boat into the water, how to reboard it, and then to find the place where Navy had taught her how to hot-wire it without a key. As the engine warmed, she walked back onto the deck and made sure all the dock ropes were released.

"Rory. What's going on?" She heard her father, and she looked up to see him a level above on the landing that led down to water level. She froze. She hadn't considered this possibility.

"Nothing, Dad."

"You are a really bad liar. What the hell are you doing?" He came down the stairs and confronted her as she continued to untie a dock line.

Straightening, she faced him. "I'm taking a trip. I'm going to TEAR. And I'm going to play the 'ultimate bargaining chip' in a place that won't endanger anyone."

Byron was struck speechless for a moment. "We don't know if your theory is right yet."

"Actually, I just watched it proven true," she said. "Which means the team can start work tomorrow on the next phases. And I have to do this."

Byron shook his head firmly. "Absolutely not. No. They could kill you."

Rory leaned on her toes and gave him a kiss. "You know they can't. They can't afford to. Remember what you told me, Dad? 'That it should be a friend to soothe the cares, and lift the thoughts of man,'" she quoted. "I'll make them release every donor, and Navy and Army and AJ, if they have them. I've got a plan. Please trust me?"

Byron's heart was breaking as he let her hop back on the catamaran and disappear inside its windowed helm. The light, electric-powered watercraft backed slowly and silently out of the dock, the last rays of sunset illuminating the subtle wake it left. She turned at the window and waved to him. How had she grown up so fast, to the point where she had become someone he wished he could have been? He'd put her through so much, and then she'd gone through more to get them both here safely. Now she was asking even more of herself.

Overwhelmed by pride and fear for her, he suddenly realized what he needed to do. He shouted after her, then ran off the dock and dove into the water. Seeing him, she stopped the craft and ran to help him on board.

As he climbed aboard the boat, he shivered, "I always wanted to make a big, heroic gesture." Rory only laughed and hugged him. "I never imagined it would be in forty-degree water. Tell me there's a heater and clothes on this boat."

Outside Woodstock, Virginia

Navy reasoned it was only maintaining the charade for him to fight back a little against the guards leading him through the compound. And if it incidentally left a couple of broken noses along the way, well . . . keeping up appearances was an unfortunate necessity.

Within thirty minutes, they had handcuffed him to a chair in a small room and tried their hand at interrogating him. He did his best to keep them fully distracted as he listened to Army's updates through his earpiece.

"Why are you here?"

"It looked like a cozy spot," Navy replied. In his earpiece, Army confirmed the layout of the building for hallways Navy hadn't been escorted through.

"Who sent you?"

"Kessler." Navy noted that their eyes grew in fear and a couple whitened. So they were quite familiar with him.

Army hissed in his ear: "*I can't find her, and I've now crossed the south half of the building. Some of it's just offices. Heading across to the northeast quadrant.*"

"What?" the guards said in confusion.

"*Oh, shit. Well, I just found the farm. It's worse than we thought, brother.*"

"How many people do you have here?" Navy asked, and the men looked to each other in shock. It didn't matter, since he wasn't actually addressing them.

"*Looks like fifty to seventy-five, all in beds,*" Army replied. "*Still, I don't see AJ here.*"

Navy scanned the faces of the men watching him. "We know you have AJ on this side of the building. And we know she's not under sedation. So logically, if I shout loud enough, she's going to shout back. Which means that will be caught on camera at headquarters and you'll all be out of a job soon," Navy warned them. He took a breath in clear preparation, then let out an ear-drumming bellow. "AJ!"

In his ear, Army cursed. "*Ouch! I told you, I get to be the knight in shining armor this time.*"

In front of him, a guard barked out a laugh. "She can't hear you from here."

Hearing it in his earpiece, Army responded with a soft, rebellious: "*HUA. Northwest quadrant. Hopefully you haven't deafened me so I can hear AJ call me her hero.*"

Navy started laughing so hard his eyes began to water.

CHAPTER 34

Off the Coast of Great Seal Cove

The dawn was barely breaking on the horizon, still no more than a blue light hinting at orange, when they passed the edge of Nova Scotia. They had each taken a break to sleep, avoiding calls from Persephone and Jeff demanding to know where they were. Rory felt it was best to tell them once they were out of reach of any attempts to reverse their plans.

When Rory sighted the coast of the cove where she and Navy had first weighed anchor, she gave her father a nod. Byron took the helm and steered for the island.

Stepping aside, she turned on her wrist phone and searched for the TEAR headquarters contact info.

The call connected. Rory asked to be connected to General Kessler.

"Um, I'm not sure if he's available. I can put you through to his assistant. Who is calling?"

"Aurora Rosalind Stevigson," she replied. "He'll be available."

Within seconds, a deep male voice answered. "Aurora? This is General Kessler on the line."

"Hello, General Kessler. I believe you've been looking for me."

He paused. "Yes, we have. We've been very worried about you." Concerned. Fatherly, even.

Rory smirked. "You'll be happy to hear that I have the answers you've been looking for. I've solved the riddle, and I'm ready to share a cure with the world."

Silence stretched. When he spoke, his tone had softened, become cajoling.

"I'm not a scientist, Aurora, but as you must know, I've been in charge of finding a cure for a very long time. I'd like you to come to my offices, meet with our scientists, and share with them whatever you have discovered. But for the sake of an old man's excitement, will you tell me what you've learned that our years of research couldn't?"

Rory nodded at her father and pointed to the cove and the dock where he should stop.

"I'm the cure, Kessler. My mother created a walking, talking wonder drug. So you'll want to write down these coordinates and get someone here fast, or I'll be partnering with anyone else who's willing to pay more."

"Where are you?" he barked. She rattled off the coordinates.

"And Kessler?"

"What?"

"Hurry. I know you have lots of birds. Send a big one."

Outside Woodstock, Virginia

Army knew he'd found AJ's room when he peeked around a hallway door with a video camera on a thin fiber-optic wire and saw two armed guards waiting outside it. A nurse in scrubs was just leaving the room.

"She's been given dinner," she told them quietly. "The meal contains some sedatives, so if you hear her fall, I need you to page me immediately. It will just make her drowsy enough for us to fully put her under the stronger drugs."

The guards nodded and Army leaned back against the wall, calculating possibilities. If she had already eaten, she'd be more difficult to move. He didn't want to harm the guards, but he would need them out of his way and unable to report back. The nurse, too.

Bluff, his mind screamed. *Easiest way is right through the door.*

Standing, he let the nurse head toward him and backed up so that, as she rounded the corner, she would bump right into him. He moved his holstered gun to the back of his waistband.

"Oh! Sorry," she said when she crashed into him, and he pretended to be hit in the ribs. "Gosh, are you okay? I'm so sorry. I didn't see you."

"No problem, ma'am, my fault entirely," he said with a southern drawl and a warm smile. "Should've warned you I was barreling around the corner. The patient named Avis James is down this corridor, right?"

She nodded and then paused, thinking better of answering as she looked for his badge.

"Ah, yes . . . but I don't believe I know you."

"Nope, sure don't. Sorry, Dr. Rajni sent me down here with a useless card, and security is still tryin' to reprogram it. I'm sure you've seen that before," he laughed with a wink. "Anyway, I guess patient James got bumped up in priority or something. I'm supposed to interview the patient about some exposures to farm animals and then travel and . . . gosh, darlin', I'm boring you, aren't I? Don't you worry about it. I'll go bore the guards down there and let you get back to work."

"Okay," she laughed, charmed. "See you around."

"I hope so. You watch out with those skinny little elbows and comin' around corners, you hear?"

She sent him a smile over her shoulder, then checked out his ass as he rounded the corner. Odd, she thought. He was armed.

CHAPTER 35

Washington, DC, TEAR Headquarters

Rory and Byron sat inside the powerful helicopter that had picked them up from the docks at Great Seal Cove. With the aircraft boasting a top speed of almost five hundred miles per hour, they were arriving before noon. Its massive, dual, forward-facing rotors below its broad top rotors had to fully stop before they were permitted to exit, and even as those slowed to a stop, the pilots told them to wait until the engines were fully off. Rory wished her pulse would slow in time with the whipping sound of the rotors, but it only seemed to accelerate.

"Don't tell them Mom's alive, okay?" she leaned and whispered into her father's ear.

"I know, I know."

"And if they separate us, you make sure anyone who speaks to you knows you've got the same genetic makeup as me and you are not to be touched."

Byron smiled at her and kissed her forehead. "You're a brave woman, Rory. You make me very proud."

Rory's gaze shot out the window at the figure on the landing pad. "Why does he look so familiar, Dad?"

Byron followed her gaze to see Dr. Rajni standing outside the edge of the landing zone, flanked by officers.

"You used to play with his son, sweetheart. You two were best pals." Byron's heart clenched at the memories of the beautiful boy who had built forts and raced down slides with her. At the memory of his funeral.

They climbed out when the officers came forward to open the doors and release a set of steps. Dr. Rajni ran forward, hesitantly searched Byron's face, and then reached out a hand to shake his firmly. After a second, they pulled each other into a tight hug.

"Jason. I've missed you," Byron said sincerely.

"It's good to see you, Byron." Jason looked to Rory, who stood back observing them. "You probably don't remember me very well, Aurora."

She shook her head slightly. "Well enough. It's nice to see you again."

"And you as well. You look very much like your mother. You have her eyes."

Rory's eyes hardened; they weren't there for teary reunions. "I think you know who I'm here to see. Will it be very long before we can meet Kessler?"

Jason held her gaze and nodded, acknowledging her demand. She wondered if he really knew that Persephone was alive. She knew that he had helped nearly kill Navy and Army. Whatever their history was, she wasn't going to trust him an inch.

"Come right along. He's waiting for you." As he led them through the building, Rory stuffed her hands in her jacket pockets and counted hallways, doors, and turns on her fingers. She hoped she could remember them if they had to try to escape. Jason tried to explain, "My whole team is very eager to meet with you and learn what you've discovered. And they're very honored to meet Persephone's daughter as well, but mostly they hope you can teach us something that—"

"Do you have a virologist on your team?"

"Of course," he answered her, surprised at her curt interruption.

"Phage experience?"

"Ah . . . no, I don't believe so. We quit all research with phages about three years ago after complete failures. It's such an outdated field of study."

"You'll regret that perspective."

Through a final set of double doors, across a carpeted office lobby, and into a large meeting room, they finally saw the general seated at the far end of the oblong table. He stood casually as Rajni introduced them.

When he extended his hand to shake hers, she resisted a shiver of disgust at the feel of his cool palm.

"Hello, Aurora. And Dr. Stevigson. Please, let's sit. You must be tired after such a long journey. You started in Nova Scotia, yes?"

"We started at our farm. But I'm guessing you lost track of us somewhere outside Freeport, Maine, a month ago."

Outside Woodstock, Virginia

Army approached the guards at the end of the hallway with a confident swagger. Though the men were armed, their guns were holstered and their stances relaxed. They weren't guarding a threat or a resource likely to escape.

"Hey," he greeted them. "Looks like he's getting bumped up in priority. I'm supposed to ask him a couple of questions, and I have instructions from Rajni to bring him up to Bethesda."

The guards glanced at each other, then back to him. He was obviously out of uniform, but the fact that he was in the building implied he had credentials.

"This patient is a female."

Army looked surprised, then gave a laugh. "You can see it was a rushed request. I skimmed it myself."

"Got transfer paperwork?"

"Out in my vehicle. We might not need it, depends on the questions." He gave a shrug and rolled his eyes. *Stupid scientists, always changing their minds.*

"We weren't told you were coming."

"I understand, but I'm short on time if the nurse gave the patient sedatives. Let's ring General Kessler, shall we?" Army lifted his wrist and punched a few buttons. Their eyes widened.

"No, man, don't worry about it. I'm sure it's fine. You can go speak with her."

They used their badges in conjunction with a biometric eye scan, then opened the door. Army nodded his thanks and walked inside.

Sitting on the bed, her legs crossed, was AJ. A plate of food sat on the table nearby with its lid off. When her eyes met his in shock, he smiled and held a finger to his lips as he crossed to her.

AJ searched his face while waves of relief coursed through her, and she found herself just as at ease near him as the first time they met on the farm. She gave in to her desire to throw her arms around him, hugging tighter when his arms locked around her, too.

"They haven't hurt you?"

"No, but I felt like they had plans soon. Thank you for coming for me."

"The phrase you're looking for is 'You're my hero.' Have you eaten anything?" he asked in an urgent whisper, leaning back to look at her pupils. "They drugged your food."

"Just an orange. I'm not eating anything they cooked."

"Smart of you to know they'd drug you."

"I didn't," she replied. "It just tasted like shit."

He chuckled, then held up a finger and glanced down as he listened to the interrogation playing in his earpiece. AJ could just see the tiny object relaying a feed into his ear canal. Navy was buying time, but they needed to move soon.

"How do you want to do this?" he asked Navy.

In his ear, Navy replied, "Quickly. I'm blowing your cover though. Keep her safe, and I'll meet you in the central communications office."

Army looked back to her as if assessing her readiness. "We're escaping. There could be some shooting, some fighting. Whatever happens, I need you to keep moving in the direction I say when I say it. Okay?"

AJ nodded. "Aye-aye, Cap'n."

Glancing to the door, then back to her, Army said, "You run a fishing boat?" She nodded. "I bet you have good upper body strength."

Washington, DC, TEAR Headquarters

General Kessler's fury manifested in the ticking muscle at his jawline. The whole room vibrated with the sense of his barely leashed anger.

When Rory raised her eyebrows in challenge, he glanced around the room. With a mere tip of his head, the officers in the room departed, leaving only Byron, Jason Rajni, Rory, and the general. After they were gone, he leaned back in his chair and steepled his fingers.

"Let's cut through the bullshit. What's your position?"

"My position?" she asked innocently.

"Yes. You're here to negotiate, let's start."

"Good. I want the assured safety of Nathaniel Vercoeur, Avis James, and Army Harrison, and the release of any patients you're holding for antibody research."

He grunted a chuckle. "In exchange for what?"

"The cure to the world's deadliest diseases."

He glanced to Rajni and asked, "Have you checked anything about her claims?"

When Rajni began to answer, Rory spoke over him. "Can your holo-projector accept external wrist-phone inputs?" She was already turning over her wrist to summon a video, then switched on the projector via tabletop controls. Within seconds, the recording of her blood cells sending out bacteriophages became a living thing on the table before them, and Rory narrated it for Rajni and Kessler as it replayed.

"Now, if you don't believe this video is real, you can have a sample of my blood to test. And I'll tell you how to structure the experiment. If you show me where you're holding my friends."

Betraying nothing, Kessler looked to Rajni. "Please step outside with me."

The doctor followed him into the hallway, and Kessler gave him an expectant look.

Rajni nodded. "It's implausible, but it isn't impossible. It's a logical next step in the coevolution of bacteria, humans, and bacteriophages. It's so simple, yet it hasn't been discovered in years of our research." He shook his head slowly in wonder. "I think she's actually done what she says and solved this."

Kessler pushed his lower jaw out thoughtfully. "Then let's show her what she wants. But on my terms. If you intervene, I'll make sure your remaining heirs die, too."

Even Rajni wasn't able to conceal the shudder that passed through him.

Outside Woodstock, Virginia

The guards outside patient James' door were both alerted by their buzzing wrist phones and listened to the shared message. They each looked to the other, realized they'd been had, and dove for the doorway. When they stumbled in, the girl was gone. Seated on the bed was the soldier they had allowed entrance, leaning over his knees with his hands folded.

"Boys, now you and I both know this could look a lot better for you if you leave with a couple bruises. Myself, I'm a pacifist," he shrugged as the door clicked behind them, "but . . . c'mon." He stood slowly as if reluctant to, and they rushed him.

Both fell flat on their faces, tripped by the line that AJ now held behind them and was cinching down over their ankles. Army helped by snapping ties onto their wrists.

"She's really strong," he explained to them when they rolled over with a moan, and he pointed to the ceiling above the door where a few pipes turned. "She was up there. Cool, eh?" He snatched their badges and handed one to AJ.

"And now for the hard part."

Washington, DC, TEAR Headquarters

Rory glanced at her father when Kessler returned and offered to take her, and only her, to see proof that Army, Navy, and AJ were safe and unharmed.

"We'll be giving you access to highly classified information. I can only break so many laws today, Rory," Kessler said. "Just you."

Hasn't slowed you down in the past, she wanted to say, but she knew it was unwise. Instead she gave her father a knowing look, hoping he remembered their earlier talk. Then she stood and followed Kessler and Rajni down the hallway.

An officer outside the door immediately fell in step behind them. Rory's hackles rose with instant alarm. There was almost certainly no way that she would remember her exits from here, and they kept going deeper into the building.

Finally they stopped before a solid metal door and used a biometric scanner to pass into a darkened room where Rory's eyes took a moment to adjust. The officer who had followed behind her stayed outside. Monitors papered the walls, and three analysts sat at computer stations before the monitors. They looked up, saw her, and each reached out to tap their buddy's shoulder without looking away from her. She recognized that they were the eyes behind the drones that had been tracking her. She wondered which one had fired a missile at Navy.

"Bring up Patient James at the hospital." Kessler hardly spared the analysts a glance; he just watched the monitor wall.

The hospital? Rory repeated mentally. *You asshole, as if you're trying to make them well again.* A lead analyst gave a gesture to one who turned and typed, then the lead explained what they would be seeing.

"The communications at the hospital are in-room monitors. It's a live feed. I'm not sure if we have audio on . . . What the hell?"

Everyone froze as they watched the screen, where a pair of

guards had just entered a small room that was furnished with only a bed, table and chair, and toilet. The view was from a camera fixed in a room corner opposite the bed and the door, so it was able to perfectly capture the man sitting on the bed. It also revealed what the guards didn't see but the analyst quickly had: the form of a body clinging to pipes in the ceiling, legs spread slightly and arms bent.

AJ. AJ was poised above the guards, and at the moment they moved on Army, she dropped in a single lithe movement, grabbed something from the floor, and yanked it up. The guards smashed forward onto their faces as Army and AJ quickly tied their feet and bound their wrists, then used their stolen security passes to leave the room together.

Rory looked to Kessler, then to Rajni. Rajni met her eyes and then snapped back to the screen, but she caught the barest hint of a delighted smirk beneath his beard.

Kessler looked to the analysts. "Well, what the hell are you doing? Bring up the whole compound!" he thundered, and the ferocity of it startled Rory.

On the screen, several rooms now appeared. Few had any movement, but she walked closer to the screen to try to understand what she was seeing. Three different monitors observed a large room, full of patients in beds spaced only a few feet from each other. Each bed had an IV pump set up near its head, the patients tubed through their noses and veins. People in scrubs circulated, checking on a few of the prone bodies. Not a single patient moved. Not a single patient's eyes were open.

The farm. She thought of these people, of their families, of years spent locked out, drugged, stolen from their own lives. From life itself. She was nauseated by the realization of what they had been through, and what they had missed.

"I want audio connection to them now to advise of the escapees."

"Yes, sir. I can get a line set up in a minute."

On another screen, movement caught her eye. Army and AJ were racing down the hallways, connecting from one monitor to the next. They encountered a couple of guards, but Army made short work of each. Then she saw him.

"Navy." It was another room, another monitor far to the side. He was handcuffed to a chair, his hands locked at his sides. In response to a snap from Kessler, the image became the central monitor's display as four guards began to hit him repeatedly, then one drew a gun and aimed it at his heart.

"Don't kill him! Don't let them kill him!" she screamed. "He's got my blood. He's got the cure, too!"

"Nice try, but I'm not that stupid."

Rory looked desperately to the head analyst. "You. You shot him, didn't you? With the drone?"

"I don't shoot people. I just oversee drones. But yes, a drone shot him."

Rory looked back at Kessler again and pleaded, "Believe me. After he was shot, he needed blood and I gave him a transfusion. He has the cure, too."

"I don't need him. I have you." Picking up the phone line that an analyst handed him, Kessler spoke. "You're holding Nathaniel Vercoeur, an AWOL Navy SEAL who goes by the name of Navy. He is extremely dangerous. If you want to control him before he cuts all your throats, tell him I have Aurora." Holding a hand over the receiver, he looked to his small audience and grinned wickedly. "This should be entertaining."

Her blood felt like ice in her veins. Kessler watched the screen calmly while her whole body wanted to scream out loud. The very reason she had thought to come here, the very leverage she hoped to have, didn't faze Kessler in the least. He would turn her into a donor in his farm as easily as he would give orders to have Navy shot dead before her. He would die. He would die and so would Army and AJ, and she would cease to live, and then the whole Resistance's only hope was to turn her discovery into a public cure before TEAR could. What had she done?

The monitor suddenly flickered, and audio came through. The guards were speaking to Navy.

" . . . have Aurora in custody. At TEAR headquarters, with General Kessler."

Navy slowly smiled. "That's okay. I think you're lying, but if you aren't, I'm not worried. She's got skills."

Rory's heart thumped to painful life in her chest, reassured and emboldened. A building alarm went off in the room on-screen, and in the split second that the guards flinched and looked to the ceiling in surprise, Navy suddenly lunged forward and spun, slashing the legs of the chair into the two guards ahead of him so hard that they slammed into the wall. She could barely track his movements as he knocked a third guard down, then sent a vicious kick into the fourth guard's face before he could draw his weapon. Once all four were unconscious, he maneuvered himself so the chair was in front of him, found their key, and had himself free in seconds. Grabbing a guard's badge, he left the room, and they all followed his movements as he converged on the same hallway as Army and AJ. They reunited with a tap of fists.

"No casualties?"

"None. AJ went fishing and caught a few, you?"

"None. Four unconscious back there. Few broken noses. They ran into a chair."

Navy looked to AJ, who hooked her thumb toward Army and said with a lopsided grin, "I'm supposed to tell you he's my hero." Navy grinned.

"Comms are this way." Army pointed to a passageway, and they followed him as Navy related what the guard had said.

"Kessler's watching. He told them to tell me they have Rory."

Army shook his head. "Lying."

In the room, Kessler thundered, "Get me audio! Get that comms room online now!"

Rory looked to Rajni, but he seemed frozen in confusion and terror. She had to stay ahead of them, maintain the upper hand Army and Navy had fought to secure. *Plan F,* she thought.

The central four monitors became one solid large image, showing a room that looked like a smaller version of the one they were in, with two uniformed soldiers working at computer stations. Navy and Army had their weapons drawn when AJ pushed open the door, eliciting the reaction they had planned for: the soldiers raised their hands in wordless surrender and were rewarded with nothing more than the indignity of being handcuffed and sat in the corner. Army immediately got to work, familiarizing himself in seconds and establishing the connection to TEAR at the same time the analysts connected to them. In a side monitor, Rory could see the room as Navy and Army saw it: she and Kessler center stage, only feet apart.

She pulled a gun from the ankle of her boot and trained it on Kessler.

"Rory!" AJ exclaimed before Navy could even speak.

"You're going down, you sick bastard," Rory told him. "We're freeing every one of those donors and giving the cure away."

Kessler spared her a brief, disinterested glance, then looked back to Navy on the screen.

"Well hello, Nathaniel. You look a lot fucking uglier than the last time I saw you. Tell me, who do you think has the upper hand here?" he said with eerie calm. "You have my donors. But I have *the* donor."

CHAPTER 36

Outside Woodstock, Virginia

Navy's gut had told him something might be wrong, the guards weren't just repeating Kessler's ploy, but when Army connected to the monitors at TEAR and he processed the video before him, he still couldn't believe it. Then she pulled a gun on Kessler, and Navy's world was inverted.

"Rory, what are you doing there?" he shouted, then turned his rage on Kessler. "What the hell is she doing there?"

Kessler smiled slowly. "Why, she came to me."

"It's under control, Navy. I couldn't let them have you, have all of you. I'm the ultimate bargaining chip, right, Kessler?" Rory asked him. To the room of people behind her, she snapped, "Move and he dies."

Kessler turned his grin into the barrel of her gun. "Well, aren't you quite the little self-aware one? What a brave little test tube your mother raised."

"Rory, my God, why did you do this?" Navy begged.

Rory continued talking to Kessler. "I won't be a pawn anymore, in anyone's game. I control the game now." When he just laughed at her, she shivered slightly.

He sensed her weakness like a snake and struck before she could see his hand even move. Suddenly the gun was twisted sideways, snatched from her grasp, and Kessler spun her in a throttling dance that left her pinned under his left arm, the gun biting into her temple with his right.

AJ let out an involuntary shriek of terror.

"Well, that was easy." Kessler's belly laughed against her back, and she read the fear in Navy's eyes on the screen before her. He looked exactly as she had felt minutes before when the gun was on him.

"Don't hurt her, Kessler. She's your only hope," Navy tried to reason with the man. In response, Kessler wrapped his hand around her neck and closed it in a crushing grip. "Stop! You can get what you want without hurting her."

"Oh, a small bullet to the brain stem will just keep her . . . obedient." With a smirk, Kessler tightened his hand, and she wasn't even able to create a sound to voice her pain. Tears slid down her cheeks as she tried to fight against him.

"*No!*" Navy screamed when he saw Rory swing an arm up toward Kessler's neck. He knew instinctively that the man wouldn't hesitate to kill her. And he watched Kessler's finger bend on a hair trigger.

But the trigger Kessler pulled clicked on an empty magazine, and her hand struck his throat right at the side, leaving a small orange tube hanging from the skin of his neck.

He was so stunned, she was able to spin away from him and back a couple of steps away as he fingered at the needle lodged in his neck.

"That's a BB gun, and it's empty," she explained of the gun through a voice rasped over a bruised trachea. "But that needle in your carotid, well—that wasn't empty. I handpicked the fastest-acting pathogen in my lab just for you: *Pandalus borealis.*"

Washington, DC, TEAR Headquarters

Rory smiled at Kessler as the injection began to take its toll, seeing the red rise to his skin.

"I thought you ought to feel what it's like to die of an infection. I thought perhaps you, more than anyone, needed to experience your lungs filling up, your throat swelling closed. Does your tongue feel thick?"

"What did you do to me?" Kessler growled, but even the words *to me* were thickened from a mouth lisping with a swollen tongue.

"You probably feel hot all over. Is it hard to breathe yet?" Rory asked with a curious tip of her head.

Kessler's hand went to his chest with a sudden wheeze, then to his throat as it began to tighten. He sank into a chair and gripped the arms of it as he tried to focus on getting in a breath.

"I can help you. I can cure you. But now I've got to hear you admit it. Admit that you had those people imprisoned in their own bodies so you could treat them like your own federal blood bank."

Kessler's eyes were bulging, his face turning dark red. He nodded. "And I'd do it again, goddamn you. For a fucking cure." The words were thick but clear.

Rory leaned closer. "And the cure? Were you planning to just give it to everyone?"

He wheezed in again and stayed silent. She leaned even closer. Her voice dropped in volume. "When the infection really takes hold, you'll start to feel like you're on fire from the inside. Like dying in a burning building, but no one will think to offer you water."

"Fuck you," he bit out, "you stupid little bitch." Then he moaned in pain and writhed, the tendons in his neck stretching up against the searing fire under his skin. Rory produced a syringe from her pocket and waved it at him.

"I can make you feel better. Just admit it. Admit who the cure really was for."

"Not you, you fucking trash! I would've let you and your worthless family die before I gave you a cure." He sucked in a breath, glaring. "The only people getting a cure are the people we *want* to keep around . . . got a whole committee of senators ready to screen out the refuse."

Rajni stepped forward and asked him, "What about me? Am I refuse? Would you have helped my family, my son?" By now,

Kessler's lips were blue. But he believed Rory would save him, and if not, well, he'd be too dead to care.

"No." He didn't even offer a further explanation. He looked away to the analysts, who wore the same question in their eyes. "No," he snarled at them as well.

Rory looked to the screen and all pretense of drama dropped away from her.

"Hey, Army, did you get that?" she asked lightly.

"Recorded in high definition video and audio," Army replied without hesitation.

"Good. Keep the cameras rolling." Holding the syringe out to Rajni, she asked, "Do you want to do the honors? Preferably in a soft, sensitive spot?"

Jason Rajni shook his head, crossing his arms. "He can swell up and die for all I care."

Rory returned her attention to Kessler and sighed. Instead of stabbing him with it, she took his arm, found a vein, and quickly delivered the medicine.

"By the way, you stupid son of a bitch," she explained to Kessler as he fought for short breaths, too weak to even speak now, "*Pandalus borealis* is shrimp. You're allergic to shellfish, so I made you a special dose of pureed prawn to send you into anaphylactic shock. This is nothing more than epinephrine. You'll be fine in twenty minutes."

"We'll get the video to the Resistance for dissemination to every news outlet immediately. You need to move, Rory," Navy ordered from the screen. "You aren't safe there."

"I know."

"Go."

She held his gaze for a long moment. The she bolted for the door.

CHAPTER 37

Washington, DC, TEAR Headquarters

Rory's pockets had held two things when she left the rig: her tiny syringe full of Kessler's special poison and her mother's security badge. The gun she had found on the boat and hidden in her boot to prepare for the Plan F that Jeff had taught her about. But the badge was the real gamble: Would it still work? Her bet was that it would, since few things were more certain than human incompetence and laziness. When her mother had died, she thought, they probably never revoked her clearance at TEAR security central.

She was right, at least for the first few doors. Her gut told her to run for the north end of the building, so she followed it. The maze of corridors seemed to have no end, and she had yet to find her father. Each time she heard voices, she opted for a door or hallway away from them.

Then she reached a door updated with biometric scanners, and she was stuck. As she turned to retrace her steps, she saw Dr. Rajni jogging toward her.

"You're as smart as your mother. But you will need this," he added, and handed her a badge. "I always lose mine when I have to go into the clean rooms, so I talked security into an extra. And these." He pressed a set of car keys into her palm.

She looked from the keys back to him and began to shake her head at the thought of what they might do to him.

"Go. I'll be in contact with you somehow. I've sent someone to take your father to my car, so you'll meet him there."

Rory shook her head in confusion. "I'm too lost to get out, let alone know where the parking garage is."

"Take that hallway, then run straight and don't divert until you get to a stairwell. Take it up and you'll come out at the top of the garage. Byron will be there." Rajni searched her face, then grasped her jawline in both his hands and pressed a warm, dry kiss to her forehead. "She must be very proud of who you've become."

"Thank you," Rory whispered, then turned and sprinted down the hall.

CHAPTER 38

Outside Woodstock, Virginia

The communications tent had been set up in the hospital's parking lot, as good a spot as any for a forward operating field base. The teams of retired military and intelligence specialists that Jeff had called in were preparing more large medical tent spaces to receive the survivors of the donor farm and ready them for transport back to their homes and families. Persephone was on the phones trying to find volunteer crisis counselors who might ease the terrifying revelation to each patient that they'd missed months or years of their own lives.

The flapping of the tents' sides hinted at a helicopter arriving, and Persephone looked to Jeff, who glanced at his wrist phone to gauge the time.

"Yep, that's them," he said to a room already absent of Persephone, who had sprinted for the landing pad of the helicopter.

When she saw Byron through the window, he grinned and gave her a smile and a thumbs-up. She could barely see Rory, but her daughter was alive. After watching the recording that Army had captured of her fight with Kessler, the fact that she had survived intact put Persephone at ease. Byron and Rory deplaned and met her for a tight hug.

"Are you okay? God, you terrified us." She ran her hand over Rory's cheek and saw the ring of purple-and-blue bruises circling her neck where Kessler had choked her.

"I'm fine. Just tired." And, meeting her mother's eyes, she added, "I'm sorry. But I had to take him down. He just had too much power over all our lives."

RESISTANT

Past her mother she saw Navy waiting for her. She squeezed
Persephone once more, then headed to him. Despite bone-deep
exhaustion, she found herself running to throw her arms around
him, and he lifted her off the ground when he caught her in his
crushing hold.

He leaned back to look down at her, taking in the dark circles
under her eyes and the marks on her neck. She was running fingers
over the cut under his eye, the bruise on his jaw. He pressed his lips
to hers.

"I really thought he was going to kill you."

"I thought he was going to give the order to kill you." She gave
a tired smile and added, "Nice moves with the chair."

He kissed her long and hard, and said in her ear as he folded
her close again, "I'm not complimenting you on your skills with a
syringe. That was a stupid, reckless thing to do, and you're lucky
you survived it." Over Navy's shoulder she saw Army walking toward her, AJ's hand in his.

"Rory! That was a brilliant, perfectly timed syringe move on
Kessler!" he exclaimed, making her laugh and Navy groan. "I mean,
like you rehearsed it."

She raised her eyebrow teasingly as AJ's pale hand released
Army's strong, dark one, and Army puffed out his chest.

"I'm her hero."

"I'm sure you are. Thank you. Birdy—I'm so sorry I pulled you
into this mess."

Birdy let out one of her wonderful laughs as she folded Rory
into a tight hug.

"Based on the reaction Army got from sending that tape to a
few reporters, you're going to make me famous. I think I'll end up
owing you."

As Navy took her hand and led her into the communications
tent, he explained what had happened during the time when she
and Byron had driven to a rendezvous point where Jeff's helicopter
pilot flew to retrieve them.

"The government is scrambling to piece together a cover to

make Kessler look like a rogue operator whose actions they can dismiss. They'll say he did all this on his own, they'll say they didn't know." He searched her expression, worried that this news would break her spirit when she was already exhausted from adrenaline and several days with little sleep.

"I wondered about that, too. So . . ." she said as she dug in her pocket and pulled out a wrist phone, "I stole his phone while he was too weak to move. There are messages with a few senators he was colluding with. I don't know if you'll be able to use it. Maybe the right reporter can make some connections."

Shaking his head in amazement, Jeff took the wrist phone and handed it to his top analyst.

"You got any more secret surprises?"

Rory took in and released a very long breath.

"No. I think I could use a break from secrets for a while."

CHAPTER 39

Stevigson Farm, Woods Hole, Massachusetts

The Jeep pulled to a crawl at the mouth of the driveway into the Stevigson Farm, where a newly installed gate with a security pad guarded its entrance. Leaning out the driver's door, Navy blinked into the biometric scanner as it ran a light across his iris. He sighed as the display screen read: *Not Recognized.*

"Army installed this, right? Do you think he set it up without your scan in the library?" Rory asked. She was anxious to see her parents after a long two months of traveling.

Navy nodded. "I thought he handled its programming for them."

She sent him a grin, then raised her eyebrows. "Maybe your viral genetic changes are manifesting in your iris! Come here, look at me closely." She held his firm jaw in one hand and looked into his eyes to see if the dark colors still fading from his skin were appearing in a new location. The colors of his eyes were seared on her memory by now. "Nope, still amber green and—" but he cut her off with a hard, deep kiss.

"I love you. It's nice to be driving back in here with you."

"Instead of escaping with our lives?" Her aqua eyes held a teasing glint.

"Your life," Navy corrected. "I was perfectly safe. Other than, of course, putting my life on the line for a smart-assed brat with no sense of gratitude."

She kissed him again, then leaned across the driver's seat and out the window to look into the scanner. A pleasant beep replied and the display read: *Welcome home, Rory.*

"Army," they both chuckled wryly as the gate opened. At the end of the driveway, her parents awaited them with warm hugs and the offer of hot cider inside.

They told them both about the last two months they had spent touring labs in a dozen countries, fulfilling Rory's promise to give lectures and leave blood samples with researchers. It was the best way to ensure that the research could continue to progress quickly, but it also satisfied the newly hired publicity specialist Jeff had assigned. He wanted to be sure that at every location, Navy and Rory were photographed and news stories were written to remind Kessler's associates that the cure would always be public.

Persephone was thrilled. As a researcher, she knew that the more labs that replicated the findings from the Hibernia, the more deaths could be quickly prevented. They shared the news that Jeff was relocating the Hibernia lab to a facility on Woods Hole, endowing a foundation dedicated to continued research into novel therapies like the one they were developing from Rory's initial discovery.

"Where are AJ and Army? I thought they would be here," Rory asked.

"They'll be here tomorrow. They stopped in with another family of survivors in North Carolina and ended up making friends," Byron explained. "Something about the Blue Ridge Mountains being beautiful with snow and Army learning to ski."

Navy chuckled at the idea of his old friend, a native of the tropics, conquering skis. AJ and Army had gone on a multistate tour to mirror his and Rory's, but they were visiting survivors of the donor farm. Rory called it the healing mission: making sure the damage done to those families he and Navy had helped separate might be repaired. Making amends. Navy had wanted badly to go along, but Rory's speaking tour was more critical. And for a while yet, he wouldn't feel she was safe unless he knew she was under his protection. Now that they were back, they would rest, visit their families, and plan their own tour. Rory told him the healing would go both ways, and perhaps he would begin to forgive himself for what he had done to the lives he helped TEAR steal.

With dinner being prepared by her parents—Byron had finally found the time to catch lobster—and the coldest days of winter blowing in from the northeast, Rory and Navy took a walk through the orchard.

"What are you thinking about?" he asked her as they walked through the quiet, cold evening.

"Nothing much. Why?"

Navy stopped and turned to frame her face in his hands. "I know that look. It's the one when your brain is working faster than you can find the path it's on."

She gave him a lopsided smile. "I'm remembering the poets my dad made me read. John Donne. He said, 'With new diseases on ourselves we war, and with new physic, a worse engine far.'"

Navy gave it thought. "So, every cure has a side effect? You're worried about unintended consequences?"

Rory nodded. She looked out across the farm, at the bare trees trembling in the wind, their tips pointed with the buds of nearing spring. "They're inevitable, I suppose. I just hope we're ready."

She threaded her fingers into his as they continued their walk. Beyond the orchard, over the eastern shore, thunder drummed low and lightning cracked the sky.

ACKNOWLEDGMENTS

Thank you for reading, for diving into a new author, a new place and time and band of characters. Your generosity of spirit is everything to me and I hope I gave back in some entertained hours. I love to hear what readers think, and encourage you to visit rachaelsparks.com to send me your thoughts or see what books are next.

I've been thinking about this novel for a few years, and couldn't seem to avoid writing about a problem becoming more frightening each year. I bow to all the dedicated researchers and activists trying to solve antibiotic resistance, a crisis that too few people recognize is already at our doorstep. Though I wanted to write, I had not actually thought to become a published writer of fiction outside my private daydreams, so I thank my husband for making a bet with me that he enjoyed losing. For giving me hope, I want to thank my early readers: my amazing mother, Deb and David, Dr. Simmons, and Susan Moeslein.

I also extend my deep appreciation to Gold Leaf Literary Agency of Asheville, NC, who pointed me to Brooke Warner and the team at She Writes Press, and to Brooke and her crew of brave publishing professionals blazing a new path for authors, especially Samantha Strom. Crystal Patriarche, Tabitha Bailey, and the rest of the PR experts at SparkPoint Studio have my humbled gratitude for helping me tell the evolution of this story.

RACHAEL SPARKS was born in Waco, Texas. She graduated with a degree in microbiology from Texas A&M University and her first college job was ghostwriting a nonfiction science book. After a decade-long career in Austin, Texas, as a transplant specialist, she joined a startup fighting healthcare-acquired infections. After relocating with her husband, young daughter, and mother to Asheville, North Carolina, she finally put her first novel onto the page. In her free time she serves on the board of the Asheville Museum of Science and loves to cook, brew, garden, and spend time with friends and family in between obsessively researching new science concepts, history, or new recipes.

photo credit: Bren Photography

BOOK CLUB QUESTIONS

1. How is a world without antibiotics likely to function? How do you imagine its impacts?

2. Why do you think Rory decides to believe she should leave the farm? Would you have gone?

3. Persephone and Aurora (Rory) have names drawn from Greek fables. What overlap do you see between the lives of Persephone and Aurora and the ancient fable?

4. Kessler is determined to find a cure even if he kills more in the process. Do you agree with that perspective? What if your own loved one, or several, had been scarred by or died of an infection?

5. Do you think Persephone's actions were justified?

SELECTED TITLES FROM SPARKPRESS

SparkPress is an independent boutique publisher delivering high-quality, entertaining, and engaging content that enhances readers' lives, with a special focus on female-driven work.
Visit us at www.gosparkpress.com

Hidden, Kelli Clare, $16.95, 978-1-943006-52-6. Desperate after discovering her family murdered, a small-town art teacher runs to England with a handsome stranger in search of safety and answers in this suspenseful, sexy tale of treachery and obsession—perfect for fans of Sandra Brown and Ruth Ware.

The Legacy of Us, Kristin Contino. $17, 978-1-94071-617-6. Three generations of women are affected by love, loss, and a mysterious necklace that links them.

The Undertaking of Tess, Lesley Kagen. $15, 978-1-94071-665-7. A heartbreaking, funny, nostalgic, and spiritually uplifting story, you'll cheer on two adorable sisters from the first page to the last of this charming novella that sets the stage for the accompanying novel, *The Resurrection of Tess Blessing*.

Found, Emily Brett, $16.95, 978-1940716800. Immerse yourself in life-changing adventures from a nurse's perspective while experiencing the local color of countries around the world. *Found* will appear to not only medical professionals but those who are drawn to suspense, romance, adventure, and self-discovery.

The Absence of Evelyn, Jackie Townsend, $16.95, 978-1-63152-244-4. Nineteen-year-old Olivia's life takes a turn when she receives an overseas call from a man she doesn't know is her father; her mother Rhonda, meanwhile, haunted by her sister's ghost, must face long-buried truths. Four lives in all, spanning three continents, are now bound together and tell a powerful story about love in all its incarnations, filial and amorous, healing and destructive.

10/18